Captured

Surrender

A MacKenzie Family Novella

By Liliana Hart

1001 Dark Nights

EVIL EYE

CONCEPTS

Captured in Surrender
A MacKenzie Family Novella
By Liliana Hart

1001 Dark Nights

Copyright 2014 Liliana Hart
ISBN: 978-1-940887-25-8

Forward: Copyright 2014 M. J. Rose

Published by Evil Eye Concepts, Incorporated

Sign up for the 1001 Dark Nights Newsletter
and be entered to win a Tiffany Key necklace.
There's a new contest every month!

Visit www.1001DarkNights.com/key/ to subscribe

As a bonus, all subscribers will receive a free
1001 Dark Nights story on 1/1/15.

The First Night

by Shayla Black, Lexi Blake & M.J. Rose

One Thousand and One Dark Nights

Once upon a time, in the future…

*I was a student fascinated with stories and learning.
I studied philosophy, poetry, history, the occult, and
the art and science of love and magic. I had a vast
library at my father's home and collected thousands
of volumes of fantastic tales.*

*I learned all about ancient races and bygone
times. About myths and legends and dreams of all
people through the millennium. And the more I read
the stronger my imagination grew until I discovered
that I was able to travel into the stories... to actually
become part of them.*

*I wish I could say that I listened to my teacher
and respected my gift, as I ought to have. If I had, I
would not be telling you this tale now.
But I was foolhardy and confused, showing off
with bravery.*

*One afternoon, curious about the myth of the
Arabian Nights, I traveled back to ancient Persia to
see for myself if it was true that every day Shahryar
(Persian: شهریار, "king") married a new virgin, and then
sent yesterday's wife to be beheaded. It was written
and I had read, that by the time he met Scheherazade,*

the vizier's daughter, he'd killed one thousand women.

Something went wrong with my efforts. I arrived in the midst of the story and somehow exchanged places with Scheherazade — a phenomena that had never occurred before and that still to this day, I cannot explain.

Now I am trapped in that ancient past. I have taken on Scheherazade's life and the only way I can protect myself and stay alive is to do what she did to protect herself and stay alive.

Every night the King calls for me and listens as I spin tales. And when the evening ends and dawn breaks, I stop at a point that leaves him breathless and yearning for more. And so the King spares my life for one more day, so that he might hear the rest of my dark tale.

As soon as I finish a story... I begin a new one... like the one that you, dear reader, have before you now.

Chapter One

She was taking a risk. A big one.

Naya Blade parked between two rusted pickup trucks and hit the kickstand of her bike with a booted heel. She turned off the engine and pulled the black helmet from her head, releasing long black hair that cascaded to the middle of her back.

The last dregs of an Indian summer lingered—the air like hot breath slapping against the face—the vegetation wilted and gasping for moisture. If the weatherman was right, there'd be storms rolling in sometime after nightfall, and the farmers whose livelihoods depended on their crops could breathe a little easier.

The rain would only make her job harder.

She dismounted the bike and hooked her sunglasses into the front of her black tank top, then ripped at the Velcro of the black leather fingerless gloves she wore and shoved them in her pack.

Her boots sent up plumes of dust as she made her way up the wooden steps to a row of identical shops, and her footsteps creaked across the clapboard sidewalk. She stopped in front of the glass doors of the diner, gave a quick wink to the two men playing checkers on the porch, and then opened the door to a jingle of bells.

The smell of grease and Pine-Sol rolled over and around her, and she felt like she'd walked back in time a few decades. The long Formica counter had pastries sitting under a glass dome, and a hand crank cash register sat at the other end. Red vinyl barstools with cracked seats lined in front of the counter, and booths with matching vinyl seats edged the perimeter. A television mounted in the corner crackled with static during a soap opera, and a single ceiling fan whirred lazily overhead.

"Good afternoon," the woman behind the counter said. "Just take a seat anywhere. It's only me working the counter today, so service might be a little slow."

"I'm not in a hurry." Naya headed to the far corner booth.

She moved with a sensual grace that had the two men at the counter following the sway of her hips and wishing they were forty years younger, and she tossed her pack into the seat before sliding in beside it, her back to the wall.

The trip into Surrender, Montana, hadn't been in her plans, but Jackson Coltraine had had other ideas. Some idiot judge in

New York had released Coltraine on a million dollar bond after he'd gunned down his wife and her lover in cold blood. But Coltraine's family had money, and the judge didn't think he'd be a flight risk. *Moron.*

She'd been two steps behind him all the way across the country, until she'd caught a lucky break just on the border between South Dakota and Montana. Coltraine had come down with some kind of virus that had slowed him down. It was hard to run when you were bent over puking every five minutes. She'd been inching her way closer ever since.

When her skip crossed into Surrender, Naya could only shake her head at the irony. She'd sworn she'd never step foot in Surrender again. It didn't matter that it was a place that called to her—that she felt at peace here like she had nowhere else. What mattered was the man she'd left behind—the man who'd made her forget that she was nothing more than a woman—a woman who had the capability to love and deserved love in return.

Those kinds of thoughts were dangerous for someone with her independence, and she hadn't looked back since she'd walked away the year before. Though she'd wanted to. And Surrender never strayed far from her mind.

But fate had stepped in and kicked her right in the ass. Coltraine was in Surrender now. She could feel him. All she had to do was find him and then get as far away as possible.

"You're a little past the lunch rush," the waitress said, making her way to the table.

Faded red hair bushed from the top of her head and her rouge seeped into the deep creases of her skin. Her eyebrows were drawn on and her lipstick was fresh and cherry red, so it feathered out into the fine lines around her mouth. She wore jeans and a stained apron that wrapped around her bony body a couple of times.

She had a voice like a two pack a day smoker, and she looked like she didn't take shit from anyone. "We're about out of everything except for cold sandwiches and what's left of the vegetable stew. My name's Gladys."

Naya's lips twitched as the woman slapped down a plastic menu on the table. "A sandwich will be fine. And some coffee."

"Tourist season is over," she said, arching a brow. "Last of the vacationers headed out couple weeks back. It's still warm enough, but the weather's about to turn. You'll need a jacket by morning. You'd be smart to vacation somewhere else."

"I'm here on business."

"Never seen no businesswoman riding into town on a motorcycle. You a drug dealer?"

"No, ma'am."

Gladys harrumphed and fisted a hand on her hip. "It's a good thing too. Our sheriff helped the DEA shut down a drug ring not too long ago."

"Is that right?" Naya had briefly met Cooper MacKenzie on her last visit to Surrender. Her first impression of him was that he looked more like a criminal than a sheriff, but it hadn't taken her long to see he believed in justice—though she wondered if his brand of justice always lined up with the law. She'd liked him. He had a quick wit and a sarcastic sense of humor she could appreciate, but she was almost positive he wasn't going to be happy to see her again.

"Don't think because we're small that we let any trouble get past us. I got a sawed-off big as Leroy's arm over there behind the counter."

"I'm sure that makes your customers feel very safe," Naya said deadpan.

"And the deputies are just as qualified as the sheriff."

"Is it a big department then?" The last time Naya had been in Surrender, there'd been Sheriff MacKenzie, Deputy Lane Greyson, and the little busybody who worked in the office and knew everyone's business. They'd been woefully understaffed.

"We've got two deputies now, and he's got feelers out to hire more, though I don't think the city council is going to vote 'yes' on that. Cheap bastards. One of the deputies is ex-military.

Doesn't say much. Looks like he'd be a good knife thrower—silent and deadly. But Lord, that man has a nice behind."

Yeah, that was a pretty accurate description of Greyson. "What about the other?"

"You sure do ask a lot of questions. I don't got time to stand around and blab all day. Let me get your sandwich and coffee."

Gladys went back to the kitchen with a swish of bony hips and a chip on her shoulder that probably weighed as much as she did. Naya had always found Surrender to be an interesting little town. Especially the mix of people who lived there. It was certainly different from her Brooklyn neighborhood and the one-bedroom apartment she rented. No one cared there what time she came or went, and no one sure as hell would stop to ask her personal questions. Small-town living and the slow pace was completely foreign to her.

Naya checked her e-mail and sent her boss an update on her progress, and a few minutes later, Gladys hustled back out with her food. The sandwich was thick as a brick and made her mouth water at the sight of it. Homemade potato chips were piled high beside it.

"Here you go," Gladys said. "And here's the check. The total is five, but I suggest you leave a ten."

"Seems reasonable enough to me." Naya slipped the

photograph out of her bag along with a twenty-dollar bill. "Do you recognize this man? He would've gotten into town sometime this morning."

Gladys's penciled eyebrows raised almost to her hairline and she slipped the twenty into her apron pocket. "Don't recognize him. But if he's in town he won't be able to keep it secret long. I did see a dark-colored SUV driving past during the breakfast rush, but they didn't stop, and I didn't recognize the vehicle as belonging to anyone around here. We've only got the one main road in and out of town, and the bed and breakfast at the end of the strip is the only place for tourists to stay. Though if he's a good camper, there's plenty of places he could set up if he's got the supplies. Rawley Beamis owns the wilderness store and sells camping equipment and other gear. You might check there too. Is this guy your ex or something?"

"He's a fugitive. And he's dangerous. If you see him, give me a call." Naya passed her card over, and Gladys didn't even glance at it as she tucked it away with the twenty.

"I thought I recognized you." Gladys pinched her lips in a tight line. "You were here once before, and damned if old Duffey doesn't still talk about you every chance he gets. Your hair is longer now or I would've recognized you sooner. Girl, you are trouble with a capital *T*."

Naya winked and picked up her sandwich. "You bet. Being

good is no fun at all."

Gladys cackled and headed back behind the counter. "Don't I know it. Take your time with your lunch."

As much as she wanted to, she couldn't linger if storms were coming, so Naya ate quickly and nodded to Gladys as she went back outside. The men who'd been playing checkers were still there, though it looked like neither of them had made a move since she'd gone inside.

Gladys had been right. There were a lot of places a lone man could hide in the area. Surrender sat nestled in a valley with only one road leading in and out of town. Businesses with matching black awnings and clapboard wooden sidewalks lined each side of the street in a neat row. The only anomaly was the large metal building that said *Charlie's Automotive* at the opposite end of the street.

The people of Surrender were ranchers and farmers for the most part. There were no subdivisions with tract-style housing. Neighbors were spread far and wide and there was no such thing as a quick trip into town. She had her work cut out for her. And if she could do it without running into the one person she was hoping to avoid, all the better.

She decided to take Gladys's advice and head over to the bed and breakfast and the wilderness store and show Coltraine's picture around. After that, her only choice would be to buy the supplies she needed and head out into the great unknown after him.

Naya looked up and down the street both ways and then moved back toward her bike. Her hands ran beneath the undercarriage out of habit to make sure no one had tampered with it while she was inside.

She felt him before she heard him—the energy spiking around her body increased the temperature by several degrees. The pull between them had always been electric—chemistry in its most basic form. But it was too late to run.

The handcuff snapped around her wrist and her helmet fell to the ground. Her arms were pulled behind her back as the other cuff snapped onto the other wrist. She gritted her teeth as the metal bit into her skin and she turned her head so she could look her captor in the eyes—green eyes with impossibly long lashes she'd always envied—and they were narrowed in suspicion.

"Hello, Naya."

"Well, well, well. If it isn't Deputy Greyson in the flesh."

Chapter Two

Lane knew the moment Naya had stepped back into his town. There was something about her that called to him, like she was a siren song and he couldn't help but answer.

It had been just over a year since he'd seen her last. Since she'd ridden into town on that wicked bike looking for her brother. Colton Blade had been in the military with Cooper MacKenzie, and he'd always told his sister that if he ever got into trouble, then Cooper was who he'd go to for help.

But Colt turned out to be a bad seed—alcohol, drugs, assault charges, bar fights…and attempted murder. Colt Blade was more trouble than he was worth in Lane's opinion—someone who'd been given too many second chances and pissed them all away. Naya knew it too. But she'd still come after him, hoping he'd listen to her when she asked him to go back and face trial.

Naya had found Cooper, hoping he'd seen or heard from

her brother, but Cooper hadn't been in touch with Colt for more than a decade. Lane had just come in from lunch to see her standing there in the office, and despite her brave front, he'd seen the despair etched on her face.

The sight of her had been like a punch to the solar plexus. Her face was a study. It shouldn't have been beautiful—not if you looked at her features individually. Her face was angular and her cheekbones flat, attributing her Native American heritage. Her nose was long and straight and her chin slightly pointed. But her eyes were what made a man lose his mind— exotic in shape and the color of dark chocolate, fringed with full black lashes. Thick brows winged above them, giving her a perpetual look of challenge.

She was tall—close to six feet—and her jeans had hugged her curves in all the right places. The belly-baring top she'd worn had shown a pierced navel, and the muscles in her arms were sinewy and lean.

He'd been struck speechless at the sight of her, his cock going rock hard in an instant and the wild lust of need surging through his body like it never had before. He'd have done anything to keep her around longer, just to satisfy his curiosity and see if her lips were as soft as he imagined they were. To see if she felt the connection the same as he did. He'd seen the way her nipples had hardened when she turned her dark gaze on him.

It had been a no-brainer to volunteer to help her search for her brother. He'd done it as much for himself as for her.

He'd never believed in love at first sight, but the moment he'd met Naya, those beliefs had been reevaluated. Their chemistry had been palpable—a living, breathing thing. And the heat that sizzled between them was hot enough to singe anyone who got too close. He'd had no control over his body in that instant, and that's something that had never happened to him before.

It looked like things hadn't changed much. His dick was hard enough to hammer nails and the feel of her against him, the challenge in her eyes daring him to do something about it, made him want to bend her over the bike, strip off those skin-tight jeans, and slide right between the creamy folds of her pussy.

"You're under arrest," he said instead, taking a step back so she couldn't feel his arousal. He didn't recognize the sound of his voice, the low rasp of desire.

"Oh, come on now, Deputy." Her lips quirked as if they were sharing a private joke. "That fight wasn't my fault, and I am hardly to blame for all the damage that was done. If you remember, I believe I was otherwise—" she took a step closer to him so her breasts rubbed against his arm, and she whispered the words so he felt them blow across his lips, "—occupied when the fight started."

She'd definitely been occupied. They'd been in one of the back rooms at Duffey's Bar. They'd started out doing body shots of tequila, getting more daring with each one. A lick of salt across the top of her breast before the shot was thrown back, burning the whole way down. Another lick low on his belly, so her cheek pressed against his hardness as she swiped with her tongue.

It hadn't taken long until she'd borrowed his handcuffs and latched him to the gold bar that rimmed the pool table. And then she'd knelt in front of him and taken every inch of his cock like it was her last meal.

He remembered the bite of her nails on his thighs and the way she stared up at him with those dark bedroom eyes—dreamed about it for the past year until his body was so hot and his cock so hard that he'd had no choice but to stroke himself to completion just so he could get some damn sleep.

"I remember," he said. "And then your brother started breaking bottles and anything else that got in his way the moment he heard you were in town looking for him."

She nodded, the teasing glint gone from her eyes. "Colt would have killed you if he'd found us like we were. I had no choice but to head him off and get him out of town. Believe me, Surrender wasn't ready for Colt Blade."

"Sweetheart, I can take care of myself, even with one hand cuffed behind my back and my cock at full attention. I'm a cop. You seem to forget that on a pretty regular basis."

"You've certainly made sure I can't forget it now. The cuffs are a little tight, by the way. I'd prefer not to have bruises tomorrow."

"I'll take them off as soon as I can get you in a cell."

"You can't be serious," she said, freezing him with a glare.

"Dead serious. I wasn't even going to bring up the fact that you left me half naked and cuffed to a pool table, but you seem to have selective memory. And well, to be honest, I still find I'm a little pissed about the whole thing."

She smirked at that, her normal good humor restored and her eyes dancing with mischief. He wanted nothing more than to bite right into that lush bottom lip.

"A night behind bars might be worth it then. I hope you didn't get into too much trouble."

"I had an extra set of keys in the pocket of my pants. Which you kicked to the other side of the pool table before you ran out the door." He pushed her forward gently so she had no choice but to start walking. "You remember where the station is, don't you?"

"Come on, Lane. We both know you're not really going to

arrest me. I've followed a skip into town."

"If he's smart, he's finding a place to hunker down for the night. Storms will be here soon. And yes, I am going to arrest you. The last time I checked, there was a warrant out for your arrest. Destruction of private property—"

"Bullshit. I was trying to get my brother out of there before he hurt anyone. The only reason that window broke was because I ducked when one of your upstanding citizens threw a chair."

"Uh-huh. Watch your step here," he said, leading her up the identical wooden steps on the other side of the street and down the long clapboard sidewalk. "Don't forget the broken bottles."

"Jesus, I'll pay the twenty dollars to replace the bottle of Jameson's I smashed over that idiot's head who threw the chair. He could've killed me. Maybe I should press charges."

"That's certainly your right to do so. Of course, we'd have to hold you in the cell a little longer while we got it all straightened out."

Lane nearly grinned as he heard her growl low in her throat. Naya Blade in a temper was a fine thing to see.

"Give me a break. This is about your ego, plain and simple. You got caught with your pants down—literally—" she snickered, "—and now you want good old-fashioned revenge. I had no choice in what I did that night and you know it. I had to get Colt out of there before he hurt anyone. He might be my brother, but that doesn't mean I don't know what kind of person he is. It was better all-around for us both to get out of town."

"And now you're back," he said, pulling her to a stop just in front of the Sheriff's Office.

He gripped her elbow and turned her so their faces were only inches apart. He felt the tension, thick with what had been left unsaid between them. "Tell me, Naya. What was I to you? A lark while you were searching for your brother? Or a distraction who fell right into the palm of your hand?" He took a step closer so her breasts rubbed against the front of his shirt, and she could feel the hardness of his cock against her jeans. "Did what we have ever matter?"

She lifted her eyes so the dark orbs were intent and focused solely on him. "You were the best thing that ever happened to me," she admitted. "But sometimes the best things come with a price. Sometimes a person's path is set before they ever take the first step. It was better that things didn't go further than they did."

The door to the Sheriff's Office opened and the spell was broken between them. Cooper MacKenzie leaned against the jamb with his arms crossed over his chest and his piercing blue gaze narrowed.

A year hadn't changed Cooper's appearance much. He still looked like an outlaw instead of a sheriff—his face scruffy with black stubble and tattoos covering his shoulder and most of one arm. He was a big son of a bitch—like all of the MacKenzies she'd met during her short visit—but there was something a little wicked, a little wilder, about Cooper that the other boys didn't quite have. He wore his badge and gun like they were an extension of his body, and the only difference she could see was the shiny gold band he wore on his ring finger.

"I've had forty-two phone calls since the two of you started walking this way," he said. "I'd suggest you get in here before the whole town is standing in the middle of the street to watch the show."

Lane inhaled slowly and then exhaled, counting as he did so. He and Naya were forever plagued by interruptions. But Cooper was right. Even now shop doors in town were opening and heads were popping out to see what was going on.

Naya turned to face Cooper and gave him a cheeky grin. "Sheriff MacKenzie. I bet you thought you'd never see me again. Miss me?"

Chapter Three

"Naya Blade," he said with a smirk. "I should've known the weathermen weren't talking about rain when they said a storm was coming." He stepped back out of the way so Lane could usher her inside. "As far as being happy to see you, I'm still up in the air on that. There aren't a lot of women I know who can beat me at pool and wreck a bar all in the same week. Looks like you're still making trouble."

"What can I say?" she winked. "I'm a woman of many talents."

"Well, I'm sure Lane would know that better than anyone," he smirked. "If I recall, you beat him at pool too."

"Don't make me kill you, Coop," Lane said, gritting his teeth so hard he thought they might turn to dust.

Cooper was one of his best friends and he'd made the mistake of telling him why it had taken him so long to get downstairs and get the fight under control. Cooper had laughed until tears had run down his cheeks, and he wasn't likely to let him ever forget it.

The station was a small square of a room with scarred wood floors and wood paneling on two sides. The third wall was dingy white and had maps of the area and persons of interest tacked to it. Two wooden desks faced each other. One belonged to the dispatcher and the other was shared between Lane and Joe Michaels, the other deputy. Since they were never in the office at the same time, crowding wasn't an issue.

The fourth side of the square room was made of iron bars that led to the cells. There were two of them, each no bigger than a walk-in closet, and neither of them saw much action except for the occasional drunk and disorderly. Surrender was, all in all, a mostly peaceful town.

Each cell held a cot, a toilet, and a small sink—and nothing else. A short hallway just behind Lane's desk led to Cooper's office, and farther down the hall was an exit door that led to the back of the building and the stairs to the apartment above the station.

Cooper had lived there before he'd gotten married a few months before, and now it was where Lane lived. It was a convenient location, but it didn't lend itself to a lot of privacy. He was always on call. But he didn't mind working. Work kept him busy. Kept him from thinking about things best left alone.

"You know what? You're okay, MacKenzie." Naya smirked and walked freely around the room, as if the cuffs restraining her wrists were no big deal. "Much more pleasant than *Deputy Holds a Grudge* here."

"If you think I'm getting in the middle of *that* particular fight then you are sadly mistaken," Cooper said. "And there's not much I can do about your current situation. You do have an outstanding warrant for your arrest, and you did leave town with a known fugitive in a suspicious manner."

Naya rolled her eyes. "Oh, for fuck's sake. You know that's all bullshit. I got my brother out of town and back where he belonged so he could stand trial."

"And how is your brother?"

"Serving twenty in Rikers."

Lane squeezed her arm gently and turned her so she could see his sincerity. "I'm sorry to hear that." He knew what it must have felt like for her to watch her only relative put away. She'd told him once she'd been close to Colt before he'd taken a wrong path in the road, and knowing Naya as he did, she probably wondered daily if there was something more she could've done to help him.

She shrugged and broke eye contact, and her voice held nothing but resignation. "It's what he deserved and probably what's best. Even though we're on different sides of the coin, you and I both stand for law and order. And we know it doesn't discriminate against blood. Colt made his choices. I'm only sorry he involved you guys in his mess.”

“We’ve dealt with it before, and we’ll deal with it again,” Cooper said. “It’s what we do. But just to be safe, I’d stay out of Duffey’s way while you’re here. He still bitches about the damage done to his bar.”

“Good grief. I’ll pay the damages just to not have to hear about it anymore. And if you don’t let me go, you could possibly have a much bigger problem on your hands.”

“She followed a skip into town,” Lane explained when he saw Cooper’s questioning look.

Cooper narrowed his eyes. “Damn, and I had sweet plans to spend the evening being stranded by the storm with my lovely wife.”

“Go on home,” Lane told him. “I’m on call anyway, and there’s not much to be done about a skip tonight. Those storms are going to be bad. Hopefully, we won’t lose power.”

“I’m more concerned about having to rescue Tyler Claremont’s cows from drowning like last time. I’d just as soon never have to go through that again.” Cooper grabbed his keys and headed to the door. “In fact, I think I’ll stop by there on my way home to make sure they’re pinned up. I’ll have Joe driving the roads tonight to check for areas of flooding. But make sure you tag me if things get bad. I can come in and hold down the fort, and I can deputize my brothers and cousins if need be for extra hands."

"It'll be fine. I was making my way around all the shops, reminding people to stay inside and hunker down for the evening, when I ran into our favorite bounty hunter here."

Cooper's laugh burst out and he shook his head. "Son, the fact that you've lived here two years now and still expect people to do as you ask them to constantly blows my mind. Surrender has a thousand of the most contrary people on the planet, and if you ask them to do something, you can be damned sure they'll do just the opposite."

"I might have let it slip that anyone caught purposely doing anything foolish would have to pay a two thousand dollar fine and do jail time for endangering the lives of rescue workers."

"I guess that's as good of a threat as any," he said. "I'm off for the night. You two stay out of trouble."

The door closed behind Cooper and the tension that had started to cool flared and simmered between them in hot waves.

"So tell me, Deputy." She watched him out of amused eyes and her chin was tilted in challenge. "Are you going to let me go so I can get a trail on my skip before the tracks are washed away? Or are we going to hunker down for the night and ride out the storm?"

A crack of thunder loud enough to shake the floor beneath

them shattered the silence. Lane moved closer and watched her nipples tighten to small pebbles beneath the thin fabric of her tank top. Her hands were still cuffed behind her back and there was no way for her to hide the reaction of her body. Her lips opened on a soft sigh when he stepped in close enough to feel the heat between them, but he didn't touch. Not yet.

"It depends." His words feathered across her lips and her eyelids fluttered, heavy with arousal.

"On what?" She tilted her head slightly and leaned in, so he felt her words whisper against the corner of his mouth.

His cock was so hard he was surprised his jeans hadn't ripped at the seams. The pounding beat of lust drummed through his body so fast he had to grip the bars of the cell at her back to keep from tearing at her clothes and plunging balls deep inside of her.

"On the game we never finished. I think it's your turn to wear the cuffs and have your pants around your ankles while my face is buried between your thighs."

She brought her hands from behind her back, where the cuffs dangled from one wrist and a paperclip stuck out of the lock.

"You mean these cuffs?" she asked with a wicked glint in her eye.

Chapter Four

Instinct had him grabbing her wrists and jerking them above her head, and he quickly snapped the cuffs around the bars, holding her captive. He tossed the paperclip to the floor and it pinged loudly over the harsh sound of their breathing.

She rattled the cuffs against the bars and arched a brow at him. "I'd forgotten how fast you are when you want to be. I bet you were a hell of an Army Ranger. And now you're a big bad cop with too many skills and no place to use them. What are you going to do with me now?"

"I've always said your mouth was going to get you into more trouble than you could handle." He nipped at her bottom lip and watched her eyes go black with desire.

"Big bad bounty hunter," he whispered, mimicking her words. "I'm going to do exactly what I've thought about doing for the last year. No games this time. No interruptions. I'm going to fuck you until this need for you is out of my system.

And then I'm going to do it again just for good measure."

She shivered and strained toward him, and he pushed her harder into the bars so she could feel the ferocity of his arousal. He felt the heat between her thighs and knew she was already wet for him.

Little mewls of pleasure escaped from her throat as the denim of his jeans pressed against her clit. It wouldn't take much to send her over the edge. But instead of giving into her demands, he took a step back and got himself under control, and then he smiled at the frustration that crossed over her face before she hid it. Turnabout was fair play. He'd been frustrated as hell for the past year.

The sight of her stretched out before him didn't do anything to cool the lust raging through his system. Naya didn't look like a woman held captive by her lover—like a woman about to submit. She looked defiant, the challenge in her eyes calling to every male instinct he had to dominate and take what was his.

Her arms were stretched over her head, cuffed to the bars, and her hair tumbled around her shoulders in a way that made him want to run his fingers through it while she took his cock into her mouth again. Her nipples pressed tight against her shirt and her breasts heaved with labored breaths.

Thunder rumbled again and it sounded closer this time,

and then a few seconds later the pings of rain hit the awning over the sidewalk. It came down fast and furious, and flashes of lightning glanced off the windowpanes, filling the air with an electrical charge that only intensified the building need.

Lane went to the door and turned the lock for good measure and closed the blinds. And then he began the meticulous task of removing his clothes, enjoying the way Naya's eyes followed his every movement and the appreciation in her gaze.

"I always loved your body," she said, her voice husky. "But my, oh my, it's even better than I remember."

"I found the easiest way to get rid of the sexual frustration was to work out. You can only beat off so many times, and it's a poor substitution at that. Believe me, I've been working out a lot."

"Are the women in this town blind?"

"It wouldn't have mattered. Like I said, anything else would have been a poor substitution. I'm too old to fuck just to scratch an itch."

He unbuttoned the khaki shirt with the Sheriff's Office emblem over the breast pocket and tossed it over his desk.

* * * *

"Very, very nice," she purred, shifting against the bars.

He was built just how she liked a man—his shoulders broad and the muscles in his chest and abs well defined, but he'd packed on a lot of extra muscle in the year since she'd seen him, and her mouth watered in anticipation.

He unhooked his utility belt that held his gun and cuffs and laid it next to the shirt. Being restrained was exciting, but she wanted to touch, to run her hands over the muscles and taste and nip at every inch of flesh. Her panties were soaked and even the touch of her clothes against her sensitive skin was too much.

There was no way to hide the straining arousal behind the denim of his jeans. She remembered the feel of him—the thick rigid flesh she couldn't quite wrap her fingers around—the way it flexed beneath her touch. Not being able to have him inside of her, to finish what they'd started so long ago, had been one of her biggest regrets. He hadn't been the only one to have dreams the past year.

Lane unlaced his boots and set them neatly beside the desk, and then he stuffed his socks inside them. His fingers went to the button of his jeans. He flicked the button through the hole, unzipping them just enough to give himself relief from the constriction. The blue briefs he wore couldn't hold him, and she saw the head of his cock peeking above the elastic of his underwear. Lord have mercy, she was about to self-combust just looking at him.

"Don't stop now," she said when he seemed to change his mind about removing his pants.

"I think I'll leave them on, just to be safe." His grin was wicked as he teased her about their last time together. "I think I should even the score a bit first."

She rattled the handcuffs again. "It's not like I'm going anywhere."

He clicked his tongue and moved in closer, his hand glancing across the turgid bud of her nipple. Naya sucked in a breath as his fingers skimmed down her ribs and stomach until they reached the exposed strip of flesh between her shirt and her jeans. His fingers were calloused and rough in comparison to the smoothness of her skin.

He tugged lightly at the hoop in her belly button. "You have no idea what the sight of this little piece of metal does to me."

"Oh, I have an idea," she said wickedly. "But why don't you show me?"

He lifted the shirt—slowly—slowly—until it was raised over the black lace that barely covered her breasts. Her pulse pounded and blood rushed in her ears as he looked at her with such longing that she was afraid she might come without ever feeling his touch.

"Lane—" she panted.

"So fucking beautiful," he whispered reverently.

And then his mouth closed over the lace covered nipple and she swore she saw stars shooting behind her eyelids. His mouth was hot, damp, teasing, so every pull and tug echoed in her pussy. She moaned and arched against him, and finally—*finally*—he put his hands on her, grasping her ass and squeezing before picking her up so she could wrap her legs around his waist. But he never took his mouth from her breasts, switching from one to the other to give equal attention and driving her wild.

His hips anchored her to the bars and she barely noticed as they pressed unevenly against her back. She looked down in his eyes and saw the wickedness there. Lane wasn't flashy like Cooper MacKenzie. He stayed in the background, an observer, methodical in his thinking. And many would underestimate his strength and power because of those qualities. But the bad boy lurked behind those eyes and the mystery of it drove her crazy with lust.

She recognized the dominance in him—the Alpha he kept rigidly under control. And she knew she was in for the wildest ride of her life. If only he'd move a little fucking faster. Lane liked going at his own pace, but damned if she couldn't try to speed things up along the way.

"Dammit, Lane. More—"

She felt his laughter against her flesh and almost whimpered as his hand came up and undid the front clasp of her bra.

"I could spend hours right here, making you come just by sucking on your nipples."

Naya groaned at the threat. "For Christ sake. I'll be dead in a few hours if you don't hurry up and get inside me."

His teeth nipped once at the underside of her breast and his hands moved down to work at the button of her jeans. Desperation clawed at her and she shifted her hips to help him get the tight denim over her thighs. He peeled the black lace panties that matched her bra down with them and tossed them both to the floor.

"Oh, fuck!" he growled as he saw her for the first time. Her pussy was bare—smooth as silk—and her arousal creamed along the plump folds of flesh.

Naya was tired of waiting. She needed to come. Now.

His cock had never been so hard, so large and swollen. And the sight of Naya's pussy and the evidence of her desire made his balls draw up tight and his cum ready to explode. He worked the zipper the rest of the way carefully and pushed his briefs down so his cock sprang free. His hand went to the base and he squeezed tightly to hold himself off.

His breath labored in his lungs and his skin was covered in a fine sheen of sweat. The storm raged outside and the lights flickered with the intensity of the winds blowing against the power lines. He wouldn't have cared if they were in the middle of a hurricane. Nothing was going to stop him from this pleasure.

He only needed a second to get himself under control. But a second was all it took for Naya to take things into her own hands. She was every bit his match, in and out of bed. He watched in aroused awe as the muscles in her arms flexed, and then she slowly pulled the weight of her body up the side of the bars.

It took an incredible amount of strength and control. His cock jerked in his hand, and he squeezed tighter. She raised herself until the bare folds of her pussy were even with his face, close enough so he could breathe in the delicious scent of her. And then she lifted her legs and wrapped them around his neck, so her pussy was completely open to him, waiting for him. It was the sexiest fucking thing he'd ever seen in his life.

"Move faster," she panted.

With the opportunity right in front of him, he had no choice but to do as she asked. He cupped her ass to help take some of the weight off her arms. And then he devoured her like a starving man at a banquet table.

The taste of her hit his tongue like ambrosia, and they both groaned in unison as just the touch of his lips against her bare pussy had her coming in a liquid rush that he lapped up greedily.

She stared at him in complete shock. No one had ever made her come like that—not with just the first touch—as if he'd known exactly where to lick and taste so she'd melt into a puddle against him. He met her gaze steadily, the green of his eyes fevered in their intensity.

"Lane."

This time his name wasn't a demand on her lips. It was a plea. And she realized for the first time since they started their game of seduction the year before that she was in over her head. Because you didn't just get a man like Lane Greyson out of your system. A man like Lane would imprint himself on your body, mind, and soul. And there'd be no getting rid of him.

He noticed the panic in her eyes and the way she stiffened against him, but it was too late for both of them. She tried to unhook her legs from over his shoulders, but he kept her anchored. And then he licked her again, slower this time, never taking his gaze from hers. He licked and suckled and tasted until her head fell back against the bars and her hips began to move against his face.

"It's too much. God, Lane. I can't—"

He heard the desperation in the quaver of her voice. "You're mine, Naya. There's no running this time." He nipped at one of the swollen folds of her pussy, a teasing sting that had shivers racing up her spine.

Her breath caught when he soothed the sting of the bite with the flat of his tongue. And then he was licking inside of her over and over again, occasionally bringing his tongue up to curl around the sensitive bud of her clit.

"You're going to pay for this," she gritted out.

He nipped at her again. "I've already paid in full. A year ago. With a hard-on and a case of blue balls I haven't been able to ease. It's your turn to suffer, baby."

And then he thrust two fingers inside of her, filling her as his mouth went back to her clit. Naya arched against him and screamed, her fists squeezing the iron bars so hard she was surprised they didn't melt from the heat of her grasp.

He let her scream. The storm raging outside matched the one happening behind closed doors. She exploded around him, her pussy clamping around his fingers in an iron fist as cream covered his hand and the inside of her thighs.

"That's it, sweetheart." His voice was hoarse with his own desire and the need to bury inside of her.

Lane unwrapped her legs from around his neck, sure he'd

have bruises there the next day, and brought them down so she was standing on her own two feet, though her legs quivered so badly he was afraid she wouldn't be able to support herself. Her head hung down, her hair covering her face, and her breathing was shallow and fast.

"It's my turn," he said, ripping at the thin tank top she wore so it fell to the ground in tatters. He wanted to see all of her, possess every inch of that sweet body. The lacy bra followed the tank top and then he cupped her full breasts in his hands, his thumbs rubbing across the nipples as she shuddered again beneath his touch.

The power she gave him went straight to his head. He pulled her arms down some, adjusting the cuffs, and then he turned her body so she faced the bars.

"Jesus, Naya." His finger trailed down her spine and she arched against him. "So fucking hot."

"Shut up and fuck me, Lane. I can't wa—"

He clasped his hands over hers around the bars and pushed into her from behind until he was balls deep. The muscles of her pussy quivered around him and he gritted his teeth to keep from exploding deep inside her. Her sharp cry was a mixture of pleasure and pain, and he paused to let her tight sheath adjust to the invasion.

She whimpered and arched, lifting herself more fully to

him and widening her stance to make the adjustment easier. Sweat dripped from his brow and onto her back, and he looked down to see his cock buried between the round globes of her ass.

"Fucking beautiful," he breathed out, his head dropping back on his shoulders.

"Take me," she begged. "God, Lane. Take all of me."

So he did. His thrusts were short and hard, powerful enough that each one brought her up on her toes as she held the bars for dear life. The head of his cock rubbed against the sensitive spot deep inside of her over and over again, a fleeting feeling of pleasure and pain that grew in intensity as he kept up the frantic pace.

The sounds of flesh slapping against flesh and groans of pleasure were drowned out by booms of thunder, each one almost right on top of the other. Sweat slicked their bodies and their breaths labored.

And then his hands moved from the bars to cup her breasts before rolling her nipples between finger and thumb. He left one hand on her breast and brought the other down farther, until his fingers slid through the cream to find her clit.

"Oh, God—Lane!"

The touch was all she needed for another orgasm to rocket through her body. She threw her head back and pushed against him so the head of his cock hit the deepest part of her to intensify the orgasm.

This time her scream was silent, as if she didn't physically have any more to give. But he wrenched it all from her anyway. He kept the thrusts going, gritting his teeth to hold himself back, so every drop of pleasure was wrung from her body before he took his own.

His balls drew up tight and he felt the tingling at the base of his spine. And then he froze, holding himself completely still as realization struck.

"Fuck," he wheezed. "Condom." His body dropped forward and his head rested on her shoulder as he tried to get himself under control. He bit her shoulder gently and her pussy contracted around his cock, making him groan with the torture.

He started to pull out of her, but she followed his movements so he stayed lodged inside of her.

"I'm on the pill. I'm safe." Her voice was as strained as his own. "Please don't stop."

He'd never taken a woman without that thin barrier of protection between them, even when she said she was on the pill. The risks were always too great. But the thought of risking it all with Naya had emotion bubbling inside of him that he couldn't explain.

"I've always used a condom," he said. Her muscles flexed

around him again and he pushed a little deeper, teasing them both. "Always. But you make me forget."

"Finish it, Lane. Once and for all."

He didn't need a second urging. He plunged inside of her like a man possessed and he jerked against her as his orgasm hit with the force of a semi. Her muscles clamped around him tighter, sucking him deeper, as spurt after spurt of semen hit her inner walls. He stifled his groan against her neck as the spasms wracked his body violently.

He'd waited a year to get her out of his system. And he realized in that moment that a lifetime wouldn't be long enough. Naya Blade was his—for now and forever.

Chapter Five

The storm was as bad as the weathermen predicted, and it wasn't expected to stop for two more days.

Lane had managed to bundle Naya up in an extra rain slicker and hustle her up the back stairs to his apartment. He'd never seen her let down her guard before. She was always so tough, so in control. And now she was a puddle of satisfied woman. He had to admit the knowledge that he was the one responsible filled him with pleasure.

His apartment was no frills, just basic necessities and no clutter. His Army days had cured him of that. He got Naya tucked into his bed and watched her as she drifted into sleep. She looked right there, and there was a tug of longing inside of him for permanence. A longing he'd given up on long ago.

He'd seen too much before he'd settled in Surrender. His time as a Ranger had changed him. Watching friends die had a tendency to do that to a man. So in a sense, Surrender had saved him once he'd left the Army. All he'd wanted was peace and quiet. A simple life with simple needs. Cooper MacKenzie had offered that to him the day he'd walked into the Sheriff's Office looking for a job.

Lane was just about to strip out of his clothes and slip into bed beside Naya when the phone he'd brought up from downstairs rang. The electricity had gone off shortly after he'd gotten the cuffs on her wrists unlocked, and they'd fallen together in a heap on the floor in the darkness. He had no idea how long they'd stayed there, recovering from the cataclysmic event that had happened between them.

The generator at the station had kicked on about a minute after the electricity went off, but he knew there were a lot of people who didn't have generators and would be braving the storm and cooling temperatures without power. Summer was officially over if the icy slap of the rain that had pounded against him on the way upstairs was any indication.

He took the call and got dressed again in dry clothes, strapping on his utility belt and grabbing a couple of extra flashlights. He leaned over Naya in the bed and kissed her forehead, causing her to wrinkle her nose in protest. Her obvious disgruntlement made him grin. Naya was a prickly creature to be sure.

"Wake up, sweetheart. I've got to go out for a while."

Her eyes fluttered open and she turned so she could see

him better. "I'm awake. I should probably get dressed and take off for the bed and breakfast. I've got to set out early to start looking for my skip."

"Stay," he said. "You're welcome to whatever you need here. There's food and a shower. And I doubt the roads will be good enough to do more than swim in the morning. We're all going to be stuck for a couple of days, including your skip."

She looked like she was going to protest. Staying the night in his bed promised something more than just fast and furious sex. He knew it. And she knew it too.

"Stay," he said again.

She finally nodded and pulled the covers back under her chin. "I'll stay. When will you be back?"

"God only knows. We've got power lines down and roads washed out. A couple of college kids coming home late are stranded out by Mill Pond. Joe's headed over there, and I'm going to go deal with the power lines. I hooked the boat to my truck earlier, so things should go fairly quickly."

"Have fun with that. And be careful." Her voice faded away as she drifted back into sleep.

Lane stared at her a second longer. He wanted to say more. To tell her what had been brewing inside of him this past year. He'd known she'd come back, because whether she realized it or not, this was where she belonged.

He loved her. He'd had plenty of time to think about it after she'd walked out of his life. They had a lot to learn about each other still, but he knew as sure as he was breathing that she was meant for him. He only had to make her come around to the same realization. And Naya was just perverse enough to run the other direction if he even hinted of such feelings. In the end, it would have to be her that made the first move.

* * * *

Naya sat up straight in bed, her heart pounding and her hands damp with sweat. The dream was always the same. She'd only been a cop for two years. But it had been two years too many. Long enough to watch her partner, Tony, gunned down for no good reason.

It had been a routine call for a domestic disturbance. They'd been to the same house more than a dozen times before. The woman never pressed charges, but the neighbors' complaints made a visit necessary. The woman would answer the door, her lip bleeding or her eye swelling shut, and she'd tell them she fell and that everything was all right.

It made Naya sick every time they took a call to that house because she knew one day the woman wouldn't be able to answer the door at all. And there was nothing they could do about it.

She'd known in her gut when they got that last call that things would be bad. Her instincts were never wrong. But she and Tony took the call and knocked on the door, just like they had so many times before.

The woman answered the door like she usually did, and Naya could see the red marks in the shape of fingers around her throat. Her pupils were dilated so they were big as black saucers, and a streak of blood was smeared under her nose. Her hands shook and she only cracked the door an inch or two. The terror on the woman's face was enough to send chills down Naya's spine. Something was different about this time, and Naya's hand automatically went to pull her weapon from her holster.

Tony tried to get the woman to come outside and talk to them for a bit without the husband interfering, but it was as if she were frozen in place. The shots that fired through the door took them all by surprise. And by some horrible stroke of bad luck, all three bullets hit Tony right in the middle of the chest.

If Naya had been the one to knock on the door that night—like she had almost every time before because she was a woman and the least threatening of the two—she'd be the one buried and gone instead of Tony. Naya had been given a second chance at life at the expense of her partner's, and it was something she'd never forget.

After the shots had fired, Tony's body had slammed back into her, falling on top of her, so she was trapped beneath his heavier frame. The breath was knocked out of her and for a few seconds, she was completely paralyzed. There was no amount of training or scenarios that could prepare you to catch your partner as he died.

Naya had still been on the ground, scrambling to her knees to call for backup, when two more shots sounded from inside the house—a shot for the wife and another the husband inflicted on himself.

She'd turned her badge and gun in that day, while Tony's blood had still been sticky on her hands. Nothing her captain could say would change her mind. She didn't have the guts to make it as a cop. But she had good instincts, and she had a nose for finding the bad guys. Becoming a bounty hunter was her only other option if she wanted to utilize her skills.

She shook herself out of the memories of the dream and looked around the room, trying to reorient herself to the present while repeating in her head that there was nothing she could do to change the past.

The rain still pounded down against the roof. It looked as if buckets of water were being poured onto the windowpanes, distorting the images in the street. Darkness still hovered in the sky, but she wasn't sure if that was because of the clouds or because it was still the middle of the night. No matter the time, she was wide awake and she might as well get up.

She stretched slowly, feeling the soreness in her muscles. Sex had been off her radar the last year—ever since she'd met Lane. No other man had measured up. She smiled smugly as a vision of his body and the thick stalk of flesh between his thighs drifted through her mind. She wasn't sure it was possible for anyone to ever measure up to that.

Her pack was on the chair in the corner of the room, and then she remembered her backpack of clothes was in the saddlebag on her bike. If her bike was still where she'd left it, that is, and not floating down the street with the cows and God knew what else.

The important thing was she had her paperwork to capture Jackson Coltraine. She could pick up clothes and other supplies anywhere. She didn't care what Lane said about the roads. The itch at the back of her neck was telling her she needed to get out there and start looking. Coltraine was dangerous. And even sick, he wasn't someone to underestimate.

Before she could get back to work she needed coffee and a shower. In that order. So she rummaged through one of Lane's drawers until she found a spare T-shirt and she pulled it over her head, enjoying that the soft cotton smelled of him. Then she headed to the kitchen to see what more she could learn about the man who'd become her lover.

The way someone lived spoke a lot about a person. Lane's apartment was sparse—only a couch and a flat screen TV on the wall in the living room. There were no pictures or other collectible type things sitting around. Her own apartment looked much the same way, but mostly because she was never there and hadn't even unpacked all of the boxes that were still in storage. She wondered what Lane's excuse was because he obviously spent time here. Cooper had said Lane had been in Surrender two years.

The appliances in the kitchen were clean and well used. There was food in the refrigerator—not TV dinners and other various dips that most bachelors would have—but real food that made up ingredients for recipes. It was obvious the man cooked. It bothered her that she wanted to dig deeper—to learn more about the man he was. But she wouldn't lower herself to snooping past what was right in front of her eyes.

That kind of personal information was reserved for long-term relationships, not lust-filled flings.

She'd bitten off more than she could chew with Lane, she thought, searching through cabinets in the kitchen until she found what she needed for the coffee. The chemistry between them had been undeniable when they'd met a year before. It had been a game. A way to pass the time before she left town again. But now it was something more, and there was no way to go back to what they'd had before.

Lane had been a constant worry in the back of her mind the past year because despite her intentions when they'd started out, he'd gotten under her skin and stayed there. She couldn't let him get too close—close enough to know her secrets and her shame. What if she let herself fall in love with him and then he ended up not liking the person she was? A person who could stand by helplessly as three people died around her. A coward who couldn't pick up her badge and gun again to protect and serve.

Naya waited impatiently for the coffee, glancing at the clock above the microwave to see it wasn't quite dawn yet, and still Lane wasn't back from wherever he'd gone. She looked outside again, hoping the rain had magically stopped while the coffee had been brewing, but no such luck.

It mattered not. She'd wait a couple hours, gather a few supplies, and then set out to find Jackson Coltraine. He was still recovering from whatever illness he'd picked up, so he'd be weak, unable to move as quickly or adapt in harder conditions. He'd be looking for a place he could lay low for a while until the rain passed and he could recoup some of his strength. She only hoped he decided not to endanger any of the citizens of Surrender. Coltraine was dangerous and desperate—two things that made for a deadly combination.

The coffee trickled into the pot, and she finally lost patience and stuck her cup beneath the drip. She took the first scalding sip, feeling the blood start to move through her veins, and then she took it with her to the shower.

The bathroom was as clean and sparse as the rest of the place—white towels and washrags stacked in the cabinet above the toilet and a white shower curtain. She turned on the water, glad to see it was more than a trickle, and then stripped out of Lane's shirt and got in, taking her coffee with her and enjoying the dual stimulation to get her brain back in working order.

She knew the moment he stepped into the bathroom. Her senses were too honed for her to not recognize the change in the air. But she also recognized that it was *him*. Her head dipped back under the spray, rinsing the remaining shampoo away, and then she pulled the curtain back.

"Holy shit. What happened to you?" she asked, her eyes widening at the sight of him. This was not the sexy encounter she'd been envisioning in her head.

He'd stripped out of his shirt and had dropped it in a sopping heap on the floor. Despite the protection of the shirt, his chest and arms were covered in streaks of mud. So was his face. Blond stubble whiskered his cheeks, but splatters of brown covered the left side of his face all the way to his hairline.

"I had to track down the truck from the electric company. They'd taken a wrong turn and had to abandon their truck because the water was rising too fast. So I had to unhook the boat and go get them. I gave them a ride so they could take care of the power lines before anyone got hurt. It's as bad as I've ever seen out there. The people without generators are going to be without electricity for a few days."

He worked at the buckle of his belt, but the leather had gone stiff and was crusted with mud, so it wasn't easy to get off. Naya leaned down and turned the water a little hotter because his lips were blue and his teeth chattered. He finally got the belt loosened and his pants shoved down. The fact that he'd left the dirty clothes on the floor was a telling sign for how exhausted he must be.

"Hand me a towel and I'll get out and toss your clothes in the washer," she told him.

"Leave them. I'll have to throw them away anyway. And I'd rather have you for company in the shower. I'll let you scrub my back," he said with a leer. It would've been more effective if he hadn't been asleep on his feet.

"You've got another thing coming if you think the sight of you covered in mud and God knows what else is going to turn me on."

"I'm not sure I'd have the strength to do anything but drop you, so I think you're probably safe."

"And the romance is dead," she grinned. "That didn't take long."

"I'll romance the hell out of you once I get some sleep." He stepped into the tub with her and hissed as the hot water hit his skin.

"Why, Deputy Greyson. I believe you've become a smartass over the past year. I must've been a bad influence. You're always so serious."

"You make that sound like a bad thing. I like to think of myself as responsible and the voice of reason."

He ducked his head under the spray of water and started scrubbing away the mud. "I moved your bike over to Charlie's Automotive, by the way. And I grabbed your backpack while I was at it. I figured you'd probably need a change of clothes. Though you might want to toss them in the dryer first as they're a little damp."

Naya's heart did a small flip in her chest that he'd thought of her. It was the little things, her mother had always told her, that made a relationship last. She found herself in a hurry to get out of the shower and back on solid ground as those thoughts entered her mind. What she and Lane had was *not* a relationship.

"Why does it smell like coffee in the shower?" he asked quizzically.

Naya blanked her face from the panic she was sure had probably been showing there.

"Here." She handed him the mug and waited while he took a long, lukewarm sip.

"This is a little weird, as I've always been under the impression that coffee should be drank while not naked and soaking wet."

"I guess it's my job to get you out of your rut and bring some excitement to your small-town life." Her hand smoothed back his hair before she could help herself. "And being serious isn't a bad thing," she said in response to his earlier statement. "I think you want people to underestimate you. You sit back and watch, and you read people fast and accurately. It makes you good at your job and complements the way Cooper works as well. He's the flash. The one who intimidates. The one they focus on while you get in and work the job from behind the scenes. The two of you make a good team."

"It's pretty early in the morning to be psychoanalyzed." The annoyance in his voice was obvious, and she hid a grin while she passed him the bar of soap and another clean washrag. There'd been parts of being a cop she'd been good at too. Just not the most important ones.

"Surrender isn't as bad as you make it out to be," he said, breaking her out of her thoughts. "It's a good place to live. A good community that cares about each other. The people here just do things differently. But mostly it's entertaining, unless you're waist deep in raging waters, listening to people who should be tucked away safe in their homes while they yell out instructions."

Naya snorted out a laugh. "I can only imagine the excitement."

"After I got the power lines taken care of, I drove out to help Joe with the stranded kids. The road is completely washed out. There's no way through from either side or around unless you go by boat, and the water is moving fast enough that it's better you don't try it unless it's an emergency. People are going to be stuck in their houses for days until it goes down, or until they get restless enough to unhitch their boats and go joyriding. So probably by noon."

Naya smiled at the obvious affection he had for the people of Surrender, even as the affection equaled the exasperation.

"Those kids were stuck on top of their car and it took all of us to get them down and to safe ground. Their car washed away about five minutes after we got them to safety." He wiped a hand over the scruff on his face. "I'm too tired to shave. Cooper's downstairs in the office this morning so I can get a few hours of sleep. We're going to be spread thin the next week or so."

Naya looked him over from head to toe, the water running over the tight muscles of his abdomen and thighs, and the very rigid length of arousal.

"I thought you were too tired to do anything but drop me?" she asked, quirking a brow at the impressive sight below his waist.

"You shouldn't have brought coffee into the shower. I find I'm feeling very much awake at the moment. Rejuvenated even."

"Yes, I can see that. Still, I'm not sure I want to take a chance on being dropped." She pressed her palms against his chest and then slid them down slowly. "I should probably take matters into my own hands."

She wrapped her hand around him and squeezed, and then watched with delight as his head dropped back and a hiss of pure pleasure escaped his lips.

"Excellent idea," he said, bracing his hand on the shower wall as she dropped to her knees before him.

She stroked him from root to tip, watching him out of those dark eyes, and the sight of her kneeling in front of him— the water raining down and droplets catching on her hair and eyelashes like tiny diamonds—had his cock jerking against her hand. Her breasts were full, her nipples puckered and pink, just waiting for his mouth.

Wanting her was like breathing.

Her tongue flicked out and licked up the sensitive underside of his cock. His balls drew tight and he gritted his teeth as the pleasure gathered at the base of his spine. When she reached the swollen crest, her tongue curled around it and lapped at the pre-cum he hadn't been able to hold back.

"God, Naya," he rasped. "You're killing me." But his hand fisted in the back of her wet hair and brought her closer. She was a drug—addictive and sweet.

She stopped teasing him with gentle licks and strokes and enveloped the crest of his cock in her mouth, surrounding him with wet heat. She made swallowing motions and he swore he felt his eyes roll back in his head as she suckled him long and slow, while stroking the base of his shaft.

"Fuck," he groaned. "Take more. Suck me down, sweetheart."

She purred around him as he tightened his hold in her hair and he felt the vibrations all the way through his body. Her hand came up and cupped his balls and he widened his stance for balance and pressed harder into the tile wall.

He looked down into her slumberous gaze and watched as his cock disappeared into her lush pink mouth. It was heaven.

It was torture. And though he was only moments from coming, he wanted to be inside her when the moment came.

"Stand up," he said, tugging on her hair.

Her nails bit into his thighs in protest and she opened her mouth wider, relaxing her throat as she pushed forward and took him down as far as she could go. It was impossible to take all of him, but the feel of his head hitting the back of her throat was pure ecstasy.

"Enough or I'll come," he growled.

Her eyelids fluttered closed and she ignored his pleas, completely lost in his pleasure. He finally gave up the battle and felt the orgasm rip through his body and down his cock before shooting into the back of her throat.

His shout echoed off the tiles and mixed with her hums of pleasure as she drank him down. The intensity of it flattened him, but he'd be damned if he was going to take without giving in return.

He pulled her head back and he felt the beast inside of him rage with lust as she licked a pearly drop of cum from her swollen lips. And then he lifted her up by the arms and pushed her back against the tile, his cock rooting between the slick folds of her pussy before sliding home.

Her legs wrapped around his waist and his arms went beneath her ass, supporting her. He couldn't be gentle.

Couldn't be smooth or show her finesse. He had to fuck her in the most basic sense of the word.

His thighs bunched and muscles quivered as he pistoned between her thighs. He felt the bite of her teeth against his neck and heard her muffled scream, but the pain barely registered.

Her pussy clenched and pulsed around him and her legs squeezed him tighter as her body burned like a furnace from the inside out, her orgasm so powerful her muscles clamped around his dick so the pleasure melded with pain.

"Lane," she cried, her nails digging into his shoulders as she thrashed against him.

He felt his balls constrict and knew it should have been impossible for him to come again so soon. But even as he had the thought, his cock jerked inside her and his cum spurted against her inner walls.

He was wrecked. Probably for life. Their hearts pounded against each other in perfect time and muscles quivered while flesh cooled. His legs were shaky, and he let her down slowly, hoping she could support her weight because he wasn't sure he'd be able to hold both of them up for much longer.

Her eyes were closed and he soaped the washrag, wiping the evidence of their lovemaking from between her thighs, and then he turned the water off. Chills pebbled her flesh and he found his movements lethargic as he reached for towels. He could sleep for a week.

"Come on, love. We'll help each other to the bed."

"I'm not sleepy," she murmured, her head dropping to his shoulder as he dried them haphazardly.

"I can tell." Amusement made his lips twitch. Naya was definitely grumpy when she was tired. "You can hold me while I catch a couple of hours then."

She grunted what he assumed was her assent and they stumbled toward the bedroom, drops of water still dripping from their hair. They fell into bed in a tangle of limbs, and Lane pulled the covers over them so they were cocooned in the warmth.

"I need to get back to work at noon," she said. "I've got to catch Coltraine while he's weak and not expecting me."

"It's too dangerous with the water levels the way they are."

"That's why I've got to go. Gotta catch the bad guys and put them away."

She went limp in his arms and he kissed her forehead while she slept. "You'd have made a hell of a cop, love."

Her breathing was even with sleep but she answered. "I wasn't a good cop. Good cops don't let people die."

And then she didn't say anything else as sleep claimed her fully, but the words she'd spoken echoed over and over in his mind. Had she really been a cop? And if so, who had she let die? His mind wasn't going to be at ease until he knew the answers.

Chapter Six

Lane dozed off and on for an hour before finally giving up and rolling out of bed.

Naya was dead to the world, but he still moved quietly as he pulled a work shirt out of his closet along with a pair of clean jeans. He laced his boots and strapped on his weapon and then went into the other room to get his heavier raincoat.

He saw the file lying on the table next to her bag and he didn't worry about overstepping the boundaries of privacy one bit as he flipped it open to the papers inside. He studied the picture of Jackson Coltraine and read through the particulars of his crimes and arrest. He was considered armed and dangerous, and the thought of Naya going up against someone like that didn't sit well with him. It wouldn't hurt to start his own search and see what he came up with.

He left her a note so she'd know he was downstairs at the station, and then flicked the lock as he closed his front door behind him. The awning that covered his doorway wasn't built to keep off the driving horizontal rain, and he pulled his hood up as it immediately battered against him.

The rain sliced at his face as he hurried down the stairs and slipped in the back door. He heard Cooper's irritated voice on the phone as he walked toward the front room. He hung his jacket on the peg and waited until Coop got off the phone.

"Damn, boy. You look like you've been rode hard and put away wet," Cooper said with a grin. "I thought I told you to take some time to sleep."

Lane felt the flush of embarrassment in his cheeks. He'd never been one to share the details of his private life with his friends.

"I got enough sleep to last me a while," he said. "Who was that on the phone?"

"That was Wally Wilkins telling me he was going to take his boat and round up some extra deputies." Cooper rolled his eyes and leaned back in his chair, propping a booted foot on the corner of the desk. "Damned fool is going to end up swamping the boat and then we'll have to stop what we're doing and go rescue the whole lot of them. He says we need more help and wants to know what to do if people start looting."

"Jesus," Lane said, imagining the worst outcome.

"That was pretty much my thought too. I assured him there was no reason for him to leave his house. He has a generator and plenty of food and water. But he told me if Rory Jenkins from down the road tried to come steal some of his provisions—"

Cooper glared at him when Lane couldn't quite hold back a snicker. "I shit you not the man said provisions, as if we're in the middle of the Dust Bowl and the Great Depression. He said if Rory tried to steal from him, then he was going to shoot him dead as a doornail."

"He just wants an excuse to shoot Rory because Rory Jr. got Wally's daughter, Jo Beth, in trouble and didn't offer to marry her. Rory Jr. ran off to join the Army instead, and I've heard it's because his father told him to take the first train out of town and take it fast."

Cooper winced and Lane nodded in agreement. If Rory Jr. ever came back to Surrender, they could have a real problem on their hands.

"I can't tell you how comforting it is to know that of the thousand people in this town, that over half of them are registered firearms users," Lane said, shaking his head at the horror.

"I wouldn't feel too comfortable with those statistics, because you know the other half are unregistered users. This is the middle of nowhere. Everyone and their dog has a gun. Hell, even my wife keeps a gun in her desk at the library."

"That's city property. Is that allowed?"

"I gave her a special permit. Considering the drug trade that was happening only a few months ago around this area, I felt it was better to be safe than sorry."

"Speaking of better safe than sorry, I got a look at the paperwork on the skip Naya is tracing. Jackson Coltraine. He's Caucasian. Brown and blue. About six foot. He comes from money, so he's not going to be used to roughing it, and he caught the flu a few days back in South Dakota. He held a small-town doctor hostage and then bashed him over the head after he gave him some samples to treat the symptoms. It's slowed him down quite a bit. And with the rain and flooding—"

"You think he's going to hide somewhere he can get easy access to food and stay dry," Cooper said, finishing his thought.

"Yeah. And with no way in and out around Mill Pond, I was thinking he might try to hit either the Coleman or Newton barns, or maybe those empty hunting cabins. It might be worth checking out."

"Agreed. But for God's sake, don't let it slip to anyone we've got a fugitive on the loose."

"Too late." Lane scrubbed his hands over his face and wished he'd been able to get more sleep. "Naya showed his picture to Gladys when she stopped in the diner for lunch yesterday. Every person I ran into last night while trying to clear the roads and area mentioned it to me."

"Great. Now Wally will want to get his boat and gather a posse to hunt down Coltraine. Damned fool man makes me wonder how he keeps getting elected to the city council."

"His mother is one of the vote counters."

"Huh," Cooper grunted. "I reminded Wally that he voted down hiring the extra deputies we need. We're all running thin around here and they're going to throw a fit at the overtime we'll be putting in because of it. I'm going to force the issue and hire more deputies whether the city council approves or not. I don't care if I have to get my whole damned family to apply the pressure. Being a MacKenzie still means something in these parts. So keep your eyes and ears open if you know of anyone who'd like a job in law and order where they're grossly underpaid."

"You paint a hell of a picture," Lane said, mouth quirking in a grin. "I can see now how you persuaded me to join the ranks." The thought of hiring new deputies made him think of Naya and what she'd said in her sleep.

"I need to ask you something," he finally said to Cooper. If you couldn't trust your closest friend, who else could you trust?

"Is this about the bounty hunter?" Cooper asked, waggling his eyebrows. "You seem a little old to need pointers, but I'll give it my best shot."

"I'm amazed every day that you managed to find the one woman on this earth who can put up with your juvenile sense of humor."

"Pretty great, isn't it?" Cooper said with the smile of a man who was newly and happily married. "I'm just messing around. Don't be so serious."

"That's the second time I've been told that this morning. I find it an annoying assessment of my character."

"Greyson, you're the best man I know next to my own brothers. You're solid all the way through, and I know I can trust you no matter what the circumstances because you see through the bullshit and you'll always do what's right. You're the person I'd call to watch my back if I needed it. And after everything you've been through, I'm surprised you're not more serious than you are. Now tell me what's bothering you about your bounty hunter."

Lane blew out a breath, feeling a little uncomfortable at Cooper's praise—and it was high praise indeed. Cooper wouldn't let just anyone cover his back.

"Last year when Naya came into town looking for her

brother, did you run a make on her?"

Cooper's eyebrows rose. "You're asking me that *after* you come down here with that bite mark on your neck?"

Lane stared at his friend without squirming under his scrutiny, and Cooper finally let out a sigh and dropped his feet from the desk to the floor.

"Give me a second," he said and went back into his office for a minute. When he came back out, he had a thick file in his hand and he passed it over. "I ran a make on her because that's the kind of trusting guy I am. And you can bet she knows I ran her because she's just that good. But I'm going to give you a little advice because I'm newly married and I clearly understand women."

Laughter burst from Lane's chest before he could control it. "I'm sorry. Wasn't it you who spent three days sleeping on the cot in the back room a couple of months ago because of how well you understand women?"

"That was a slight—setback," Cooper said with a wry smile. "I've also learned all about compromise, and I'm going to tell you straight out not to look in that file if you care for her as much as I think you do."

Lane let out a breath he hadn't known he'd been holding. "I think I have to look. She mentioned something earlier. That she was a cop. That she'd let people die."

"Ask her about it," Coop repeated.

"You told me that I cut through the bullshit and that you always know I'm going to do what's right. I do care about her. But I need to know if my instincts are off on this one and she's not the woman I think and hope she is."

Cooper sighed and handed him the file, and Lane weighed it in his hands, knowing what he found inside could change everything. Or nothing. He flipped it open without regrets and was greeted by the sight of her picture taken at the academy. She looked much the same as she did now, only there was a naivety in her eyes in the photograph that had long since been lost.

He read the overview of her short career and how it had ended, and his heart broke for her because obviously she was still suffering from the loss of her partner and the victim. She'd had no family left to lean on, and he couldn't imagine that her line of work let her have time for close friends or lovers.

"You should have listened to MacKenzie's advice," Naya said in a voice cold enough to give him frostbite. "If I'd wanted you to poke through my personal life, I would've given you the file myself."

Chapter Seven

Lane and Cooper both looked up sharply because Naya had managed to get past both of their guards. She hadn't made a sound coming through the back door, and there was no telling how much of their conversation she'd overheard.

Cooper felt bad for his friend. If looks could've killed, Lane would be six feet under. One of the things he'd always appreciated most about Lane was his ability to never let others see what he was feeling or thinking. If the death rays Naya was shooting from her eyes bothered Lane in any way, he wasn't showing it.

"I saw a couple of boats hitched up to pickup trucks out back," she said, turning her attention to Cooper. "Any chance I could borrow one so I can start tracking my skip? I'm thinking he's probably hiding in a barn or an empty house. And he would've tried to get as far outside of town as possible before the storm hit to reduce his chances of being seen."

Cooper looked between Lane and Naya, both of them working so hard at trying to hide what they were feeling that they were missing what was staring them in the face. He let out a breath and decided he was too old for this. He'd found his woman. Everyone else was on their own.

"Yeah, that's the same conclusion we came up with." Cooper moved to the maps tacked onto the wall and pointed to a spot with his finger. "These are your two most likely areas. He would've had a lot of miles to cover before the storm hit. Surrender is bigger in square miles than it looks, and the ranches cover hundreds of acres. The next town over is Myrna Springs, but it's another two-hour drive with nothing in between, so I doubt he'd have kept going before the storm hit."

"Any empty buildings in that area?" she asked.

"A few. Mostly old hunting cabins and a couple of abandoned barns. The people around here know flooding is a possibility during the rainy season so houses are built up on higher ground. The barns too. It's just the overflow from the lakes that make the roads flood like this."

"What was he driving?" Lane asked, moving to stand beside them so he could see the maps.

Naya kept her gaze on the map, trying to run scenarios in her head while not letting how close Lane was standing to her make her uncomfortable. "He stole a dark blue Tahoe in South Dakota. I found a gas station attendant who remembered seeing it once we crossed the border into Montana, and Gladys from the diner remembered seeing a dark SUV driving through town yesterday morning. There aren't a lot of places to stop out here for him to boost another, so I have to assume he's still driving the Tahoe."

"Any word of an abandoned vehicle sighting?" he asked Cooper, since he'd been on call all morning.

"Nothing yet. But sometimes those back roads don't have a car on them for days. There are hunting cabins here and here," Cooper said, circling the spots on the map. "One of them is in the flood zone, so unless he's an idiot, he's probably not camped out there. But the other one has possibilities. You'll definitely need a boat to get there though."

"I'll take her," Lane said. "You've got Wally and his posse to deal with."

"Thanks for reminding me," Cooper said dryly. "Maybe I'll just get them all to meet me at Duffey's and get them drunk so I can arrest them."

"You always have the best ideas. I guess that's why you make the big bucks."

Cooper grinned and slapped Lane on the shoulder.

"I don't mean to interrupt your male-bonding time, but I

don't need a guide. I can take the boat and be back before it gets dark."

"Sorry, sweetheart. Those vehicles are police property. So that means you're stuck with me."

Her smile was sharp as a blade, and Lane felt the cut from where he stood. "Let's get moving then. If we're lucky, I can be back in New York by this time tomorrow." The words were meant to slice, as if what they'd shared between them had been nothing.

"Let's get moving then. I'd hate to get in your way." Lane grabbed his rain jacket and tossed a spare to Naya, and then he dug around in the closet for rain boots that came up to the knee. "You'll need these or you'll be looking for your shoes in the muck."

"You guys don't mind me," Cooper said, taking a seat in Lane's desk chair. "I'm just going to sit back and enjoy the show."

"I'm certainly glad it's not illegal for me to do this," Naya said, flipping up her middle finger at Cooper. He cracked out a laugh as she tossed the door open and stepped out onto the sidewalk.

"I couldn't have said it better myself," Lane said, following her out into the storm.

* * * *

Water and mud slushed up from the tires of his Bronco and the wipers swished frantically in the thankless task of clearing the windshield.

The trek from downtown Surrender to the country roads was a slow and painstaking process. Limbs had fallen across the roads, and debris, like trashcans and other items found in yards, had been carried some distance from their homes.

"Why did you say you hadn't been a good cop?" Lane asked, breaking the silence since it looked like they were going to be stuck together for a while. "I know you're pissed that Cooper ran a background check on you and that I read it, but I didn't see anything in that paperwork that said you'd been anything other than good at your job."

"You had no right looking into my private life. And I know what kind of cop I was better than anything written in those papers. But it's done, Lane. And I don't want to talk about it or rehash the past."

She turned her head and looked out the side window, and Lane gripped the steering wheel a little tighter in frustration. Also in trepidation, because what he was about to say hadn't been spoken before. Not even to Cooper.

"I was career military," he said softly, his voice barely audible over the rain. "I'm thirty-six, by the way. I enlisted just after 9/11 and hit the ground running. I was a Ranger, so my unit was put in some pretty sticky situations. Over and over again we'd be deployed and come back as a whole unit. When my commanding officer took retirement, his job was offered to me."

Naya had turned some in her seat so her attention was focused on him. Lane kept his eyes on the road, sticking toward the high ground and looking for a good place to unhitch the boat. They wouldn't be dry and warm for much longer.

"It's harder when you're in command," he said. "The sense of responsibility weighs on you. Your only thought going in and out is to make sure your men survive and to leave no one behind. Three years ago my unit was deployed to Kandahar, Afghanistan. There were eight of us doing a routine sweep when we heard yells—terrified screams of women and children and shouting from men. Militant leaders had set a trap for us, using children as bait, though we didn't know at the time that the children were their own—ones they were already training to join their ranks."

He felt the sympathy—the pity—in her stare, but she remained silent.

"The terrorists had gathered the children in the middle of the street, holding guns to their heads while they yelled for us to come out and see what we had caused. My men followed procedure and surrounded them. My sharpshooters were in place, and I'd called for an extra unit to come back us up. But one of my rookies didn't cover himself as he should have—a simple mistake he'd never get the chance to correct. They'd placed shooters at the top of the buildings to pick us off, and they took the shot as soon as they saw him."

Lane would've given anything for a drink—something to wet his throat so the words came out easier, and something to burn on the way down so it reminded him he was still alive. But there was nothing, so he forged ahead.

"All hell broke loose. Bullets flying from every direction. There was nothing to do but cover and wait for help to arrive. By the time it was over, I'd lost all but two of my men."

"I'm sorry," she whispered.

"I could've made different choices," he said, pulling the truck to a stop and backing up to position the boat. "It's torture to hold command, to make choices and demand that your men continue to follow orders even when they're dropping like flies around you. The two who survived—"

He paused and turned off the engine, the silence deafening as he gathered his thoughts. "We managed to regroup and stick together until the backup units came to lay down cover so we could get out. But we watched as the ones firing at us began to seek out the fallen soldiers and gather their bodies in a pile. They doused them with gasoline and set them on fire while we stayed hidden—helpless to do anything about it." His breath was controlled as he let it out softly. "Make sure your men survive and leave no one behind. I failed on both accounts."

She reached out hesitantly and took his hand, squeezing it gently. "I understand what you're saying, and I know this wasn't easy for you to tell me. Why did you?"

"Because I understand what it's like to feel like you didn't do enough. And I understand what it feels like to have no one around to bring you out of the abyss and the nightmares when things get bad. I didn't have a family to come home to. I was an only child and my parents died in a car wreck when I was seventeen. And after the mission in Kandahar was finished and I'd turned in my retirement papers, I pretty much roamed aimlessly for an entire year, living off my pension and traveling from place to place. And then one day I found myself in Surrender and I met Cooper MacKenzie. Before I knew what was happening, the people here became a kind of family, and I found the guilt of surviving didn't weigh quite as heavily as it once had. I'm saying it doesn't hurt to lean on someone every once in a while."

Chapter Eight

Lane's words ate at her while they worked to unhitch the boat and get it into the water. The rain jacket and boots hadn't helped much. They were both soaked to the skin by the time they got into the boat and Lane started the engine.

She didn't have the luxury of falling into a town and job that could become her family. Her brother was in prison, her mother was dead, and her dad had left for parts unknown when she'd barely been walking. Her neighbors didn't know her and there were so many people in New York, no one glanced her way as she walked down crowded sidewalks. She was utterly alone. And maybe what Lane said was right. Maybe the dreams wouldn't be so hard to bear if there was someone to hold her when she woke from them.

Lane steered the boat with expertise, and she had to admit she was glad he'd come along with her. She wouldn't have gotten very far in unfamiliar territory in these kinds of conditions. Limbs swirled in the fast-moving brown water where the roads had once been.

"Look there," she said, pointing through the trees some distance away. It was hard to be sure of the color, but a vehicle had been overturned by the water and only the tail end was visible.

"Let me see if I can get closer. There are too many trees to maneuver through." Limbs scraped along the bottom of the boat, and Naya pulled her hood around her face to keep the rain out so her vision was clear.

"Could be it. I think it's dark blue, but it could be black."

"Close enough for us to check it out. The first hunting cabin is just up the way."

He put the boat in reverse and headed back to the main road, and Naya dug in her bag for her extra cuffs and the homemade weapon she used to stop the skips who wanted to run.

"Whoa! What the hell is that?" Lane asked, looking very nervous all of a sudden.

Naya grinned and held up the modified sawed-off shotgun. "It shoots sandbags," she explained. "It doesn't hurt the skips too bad, but it doesn't feel real good either when one hits them in the chest with that much force."

"I can imagine. I'll pretend I didn't see that. I'm almost

positive it's not legal."

"Sure it is. And pretty damned effective too. I only have to shoot once and it knocks them on their ass. Then all I have to do is slap on the cuffs."

"We're going to have to talk about this fascination you have with handcuffing people," Lane said, arching a brow at her.

She felt her lips twitch and looked the other way so he wouldn't see. She wanted to be mad about him invading her privacy. If she was mad, it'd be easier to walk away. To go back to being alone with a justified reason.

They almost missed the hunting cabin because of a tree that had been knocked over, blocking it from sight.

"Well, I don't think he's staying there." Lane idled the boat a few feet away. "This is residual from the lake runoff. The cabin is in the flood zone, which is why no one uses it anymore. It's just a one-room shack like most of the hunting cabins around here, so what you see is what you get."

Water rushed through broken-out windows and the door hung on one hinge, banging back and forth against the cabin as the water pushed past it.

"Let's head to the other one," she said, starting to feel the prickle of unease at the base of her neck. She gripped her weapon tightly as Lane nodded and drove the boat farther up the road.

"We'll have to get out here and walk to land level," he said, docking by a tree. "The other cabin is on higher ground."

Naya was glad Lane had loaned her the boots when she rolled out of the boat and into water that hit just below her knees. The temperature had dropped steadily and it didn't help that her jeans were soaking wet and her hair plastered to her head, snaking beads of frigid water down the collar of her shirt.

Lane took her arm and they waded to higher ground. Their boots sucked at the mud and the slight incline was slippery enough that she lost her balance a couple of times and had to grab Lane's shoulder to keep from falling.

"Stay low here," he whispered. "The cabin is just over this rise and there isn't a lot of cover if you come at it direct. We'll split off in either direction and come at it from the sides."

It was easy for her to picture him as a commander. His orders were precise and direct, and he had no doubt that they'd be followed to the letter. She nodded and watched his fingers as they counted to three and then gave the "go" sign. Naya crouched low and moved from tree to tree, using them as cover, though she wasn't sure anyone would be able to see that far from the cabin because of the heaviness of the rain.

Her heart thudded in her chest as the little cabin came into view. He was in there. She knew it. Could feel it. No lights showed from the inside, but Coltraine would keep it dark if he suspected someone was outside trying to look in.

She'd be the most exposed on her run from where she was hidden to the side of the cabin. The rain made everything more difficult—more dangerous. She caught movement on the opposite side of the cabin and saw Lane move into position similar to how she was. And then he gave the signal to go and they both ran up to the sides of the cabin, staying low and against the wall once they got there.

There was no back door in a one-room hunting cabin, so they had no choice but to go through the front. She crept around the side of the house and met Lane at the front door, his weapon down at his side. Visions of the last time she'd stood in front of an unknown threat with someone she cared about flashed through her mind and she grabbed Lane's arm, squeezing so he would know to let her go in first.

He looked down at where her hand rested and then back at her face and shook his head. She could see the compassion, but also the steel behind it. Lane would never let someone walk through the door in front of him. It wasn't in his nature.

"On three," he mouthed. "You go low. It'll be fine, love."

He started the count and on three his foot slammed into the door, knocking it back on its hinges. She went in low, her makeshift weapon ready to fire if need be. The first thing she noticed was the smell. Bitter sickness filled the air and she brought her arm over her nose and mouth to block it.

A low moan sounded from the corner of the room, and she and Lane both turned in unison and pointed their weapons at Jackson Coltraine. He was at least twenty pounds lighter then he'd been when he'd left New York a month ago. His face was gaunt and dirty and his clothes ragged. He lay huddled in the corner, and his eyes burned bright with fever.

"Just take me," he said, holding out shaking hands in surrender. "I'm fucking sick. Get me a doctor. Take me in."

"Jesus," Lane said, his mouth tightening in a thin line. "That's just pathetic. Let's get him back to the boat and into town. He can spend the night in jail while we get Doctor MacKenzie to come out and take a look at him. It'd be a shame for him to die before he was able to go to trial."

"It'd at least save some taxpayer money."

"Are you two going to shut up and arrest me or not? I think I might need to throw up again."

"I'll let you take point here," Naya said, elbowing Lane in the side. "You've got the badge."

"You'll owe me one."

"That never turns out to be a bad thing," she winked.

"I said arrest me already! This is police brutality, having to listen to you yammer on."

"Shut up, Coltraine," Lane said, pulling him to his feet and slapping cuffs on. "And if you throw up in my boat, you're going to be sorry."

Chapter Nine

Cooper handed her a cup of hot coffee. They'd brought Coltraine back into town and gotten him behind bars. Coltraine wasn't someone to be trusted, and she didn't want to see anyone hurt because they'd let their guard down. Coltrain might be sick and weak, but he was still dangerous.

She warmed her hands on the cup and didn't care that her chattering teeth knocked against the cup every time she tried to take a drink. Thomas MacKenzie had already been in town helping his brothers make things more organized and assisting those who were without electricity, so they hadn't had to wait long for him to make his way to the jail.

"You should get a shower and get warm," Lane said, coming up beside her. He held his own cup of coffee and his clothes were as soaked as hers. "He's not going anywhere for a while."

"Do me a favor and go into the cell with Doctor

MacKenzie. I don't trust Coltraine."

"I can do that. If you'll go up and stop being so stubborn." He handed her his keys so she could get inside. "Your lips are blue."

Naya rolled her eyes and headed down the hall toward the back door and then up the stairs to the apartment. Her time in Surrender was running out. She shouldn't feel such panic at the thought of leaving. This wasn't her home. But Lane was here. And the thought of going home to her own empty apartment wasn't at all appealing.

She'd spent her life on her own, never needing anyone. Her partner had been the closest thing she'd had to a mentor and friend, and he'd died right in front of her eyes. She always thought of his death as a kind of payback for letting herself care for him. Everyone close to her in her life had abandoned her. But the thought of Lane doing the same made her heart hurt. It was why it was best she suck it up and leave before she had to face the disappointment.

She showered quickly and changed into a pair of Lane's sweats she'd found in his drawer. They were much too big for her, but they were warm, which was all she cared about. She brushed the tangles from her hair and left it to dry around her shoulders, and then went into the living room where her belongings were stashed.

She didn't have much to pack, hardly anything at all, but she went through the process anyway to make her leaving more permanent in her mind. She'd set the bags on the table and gone to the kitchen to make more coffee when she heard the knob turn and Lane come in.

His eyes automatically went to her bags and then his heated gaze found her. He stared at her a few seconds, and she wondered what was going through his mind.

"I'm going to grab a quick shower. There's sandwich stuff in the fridge if you're hungry."

She assumed that meant he wanted a sandwich too, so once he went into the bedroom, she started assembling ingredients on the counter. When he came back ten minutes later, Naya's mouth went dry and her throat closed at the sight of him. He wore only a towel tied precariously at his hips.

The knife she'd picked up to cut the sandwiches clattered to the counter, and she forgot what she was doing—that she was trying to keep her distance.

"I—your sandwich. It's ready."

He smiled but didn't say anything as he came toward her. Her nipples hardened against the soft texture of the sweatshirt she wore and her breasts felt heavy. Liquid desire gathered between her thighs and the pulse in her throat jumped as his hand reached out to touch the side of her face.

"Lane—"

"Ssh, sweetheart. Just kiss me." His lips touched the corner of her mouth and then trailed lightly over her jawline.

"This is a mistake," she managed to get out as his teeth tugged at the lobe of her ear. "Don't make this harder than it has to be."

"Why would I make it easy?"

She didn't have an answer to that question. She only knew he'd ruin her if he touched her again. Her hands came up and rested against his chest, the silky hairs tickling her palms, and she meant to push him away. But he moved in, trapping her against the counter so she felt his hard cock pressing against her stomach through the towel.

"Just a kiss, Naya."

It seemed unreasonable to deny him such a simple request. His thumb brushed across her bottom lip once, making her tremble. She'd never trembled for any man. And then his lips touched hers and she was lost in the sensation. This man belonged to her—he was the part of her that had been missing all these years.

He pulled the sweatshirt over her head and jerked the sweatpants down her hips. The towel he wore fell to the floor, rasping over her skin as it went down, but his mouth continued to work its magic, slanting over her lips while his tongue danced erotically against hers.

His hands were gentle, the complete opposite of the need she felt building inside of him and the way his cock pressed against her stomach and branded her with its heat.

He surprised her by picking her up in his arms and carrying her to the bedroom, closing the door behind him with his foot. He laid her on the bed gently, following her down and settling between her thighs while he continued to kiss her. His hands were broad and rough as they made their way over her body, touching every inch of her skin, heating her from the inside out and driving her wild.

The change between them was palpable—panic inducing— and for a moment she wasn't able to breathe as emotions swept through her. It would be easier if he took her as he had before, if it was hands and mouths and a fast coupling that could camouflage the feelings wreaking havoc on her heart and mind.

She needed to touch him. Her hands came up to his shoulders, testing the strength of them before skimming her nails lightly down to the center of his back. Her neck arched as his lips suckled at the sensitive flesh there and she opened her legs, wrapping them around his hips while he slid the rigid stalk of his cock between her bare folds, probing at her entrance.

He didn't enter her—not yet. But he teased them both, heightening the pleasure and prolonging it while they memorized every inch of one another.

"Lane—" she moaned.

"Look what we have, Naya. Would you deny it? Would you run from it?"

She shook her head against the pillow. It was too late for her to deny anything. And she was no longer sure she had the strength to walk away, even as she resigned herself to getting her heart broken once more by someone she loved. *Love.* God, how had that happened?

"Please, Lane. Just love me."

"I am," he whispered. "I do."

And then she felt him probing at her vagina just before he slid inside, his movements slow and easy—tender. She arched against him, accepting all of him, and she wrapped her arms around him in an embrace as he began to move. A slow rocking of flesh against flesh that prolonged the tension building inside of her, so it kept her hovering just on the edge of fulfillment.

"Look at me, Naya," he said, grasping her hands and holding them on either side of her head.

Her eyelids grew heavy, and her whole body arched in anticipation, as if it were on the precipice ready to fall into oblivion. She looked into his eyes and fell deep into his gaze, and then her body clenched and her pussy convulsed as the orgasm rolled through her like a wave. His eyes went opaque and he jerked against her just before he followed her over the edge.

He rolled to his side and brought her with him so she was snuggled close. His heart pounded against her hand and their bodies were damp with sweat.

"I love you," he said, kissing her forehead. "I loved you a year ago when I first met you."

A joy so profound she wasn't sure she could contain it all filled her, and all she could do was hold him tighter. She couldn't speak. And she didn't see the sadness in his eyes when she didn't return the words.

Chapter Ten

The next morning came sooner than Lane wanted. During the night, he and Naya had made love multiple times, turning to each other over and over again. He'd thought she'd eventually say the words he needed to hear, but she never did. But it had *felt* like she loved him every time she touched him, loving him with her mouth and hands and body.

But as soon as the first hint of sunlight peeked through the bedroom window, it was as if the night had never happened. She'd rolled out of bed and dressed, stopping only long enough to make the coffee she seemed to need to survive.

He pulled on a pair of sweats and followed her to the kitchen, wondering how to say what he wanted without scaring her more than he already had.

"Stay," he said. "Don't go back to New York."

She looked up at him in surprise. "I've got to take Coltraine back and get him booked."

"I told you I loved you."

"I know. I love you too. You've made me realize I've kept myself closed off, not letting people in because I've been too afraid of getting hurt."

"So is that it? You've realized what you've been missing and now you're just going to go back to New York and leave Surrender behind? Can you really do that? Just walk away without giving it a chance? Surrender healed me when nothing else would. But I'd leave in a heartbeat if it meant I got to spend another day—another lifetime—with you."

His breathing was harsh and something that felt an awful lot like fear clutched at his belly when he saw the look of surprise on her face. He could feel her slipping out of his grasp like grains of sand.

"And I know I don't have the right to ask, but I'm going to anyway because I've got nothing left to lose. Could you stay? Could you be happy here? Leave the city and your job and your friends for a small town with a bunch of people who will want to know every inch of your past, present, and future?"

She clasped her hands in front of her and took a step closer, her gaze never straying from his. "No," she finally said. "I couldn't stay here for that reason."

Lane felt as if someone had just knifed him in the gut and he was bleeding to death. His body was numb. He'd laid himself bare and she'd rejected him. And dammit, he wouldn't do it again. He had his pride. He nodded stiffly and then turned away to head back to the bedroom. If he didn't escape now he'd end up on his knees begging.

"I couldn't stay here for them," she said before he could get away. "But I could stay here for you. I *will* stay here for you. I told you I loved you too. I meant it. I've been without a family for too long. Be mine."

He felt the smile spread across his face. "Is that a proposal?"

"No, but I'll say yes when you decide to ask me."

He opened his arms, waiting, and then he let out the breath that had been trapped in his lungs as she walked into his embrace.

"It turns out Surrender is in need of another good cop. What do you say to that?"

"I say one step at a time, Deputy Greyson. One step at a time. But feel free to love me in the meantime."

"Always," he said, leaning down to seal the deal with a kiss.

Sign up for the 1001 Dark Nights Newsletter
and be entered to win a Tiffany Key necklace.
There's a new contest every month!

Visit www.1001DarkNights.com/key/ to subscribe.

As a bonus, all subscribers will receive a free
1001 Dark Nights story on 1/1/15.
The First Night
by Shayla Black, Lexi Blake & M.J. Rose

Turn the page for a full list of the
1001 Dark Nights fabulous novellas...

1001 Dark Nights

FOREVER WICKED
A Wicked Lovers Novella
by Shayla Black

CRIMSON TWILIGHT
A Krewe of Hunters Novella
by Heather Graham

CAPTURED IN SURRENDER
A MacKenzie Family Novella
by Liliana Hart

SILENT BITE: A SCANGUARDS WEDDING
A Scanguards Vampire Novella
by Tina Folsom

DUNGEON GAMES
A Masters and Mercenaries Novella
by Lexi Blake

AZAGOTH
A Demonica Novella
by Larissa Ione

NEED YOU NOW
by Lisa Renee Jones

SHOW ME, BABY
A Masters of the Shadowlands Novella
by Cherise Sinclair

ROPED IN
A Blacktop Cowboys ® Novella
by Lorelei James

TEMPTED BY MIDNIGHT
A Midnight Breed Novella
by Lara Adrian

THE FLAME
by Christopher Rice

CARESS OF DARKNESS
A Phoenix Brotherhood Novella
by Julie Kenner

Also from Evil Eye Concepts:
Tame Me
A Stark International Novella
by J. Kenner

Acknowledgements from the Author

Thanks to my readers who keep asking for more MacKenzies. This is for you. And thanks to Liz and MJ for inviting me to be a part of this amazing project.

About Liliana Hart

Liliana Hart is the *New York Times* and *USA Today* Bestselling Author of more than twenty-five novels. She lives in Texas in a big, rambling house, and she's almost always on deadline. She loves to hear from readers.

Sizzle

The MacKenzie Family
By Liliana Hart
Now Available!

The next installment of the bestselling MacKenzie Series…

A killer who taught her everything she knows…
A mission that pits her skills against his…
And a new partner that makes her body…Sizzle

When Declan MacKenzie asks Archer Ryan to do a special job for MacKenzie Security, Archer has no choice but to say yes. He owes Declan his life, and Declan more than has his hands full with his own family problems. Little does Archer know he'll be chasing a would-be recruit all the way to hell and back. Or maybe Alaska just seems like hell.

Audrey Sharpe works for no one but herself. Not even when the most elite security company in the country wants her. She doesn't have time to worry about MacKenzies. She's racing against the clock to hunt down the man who taught her everything she knows and to stop him from killing more innocent people. When sexy, but tough as nails, Archer Ryan keeps getting in her way, Audrey has to decide whether he'll be an asset or a distraction her body and mind can't afford.

* * * *

Hospitals reminded him of death—the cloying antiseptic that didn't quite mask the bitter smell of urine and blood, and the insistent beep of machines that pumped life into the fragile human body.

When it came his time to go, he'd rather be taken out swiftly—in the line of duty preferably—without having to linger and waste away while a machine allowed him a few more precious breaths.

Archer Ryan waited patiently as the elevator rose to the top floor, his hands relaxed by his sides, and none of the nerves he felt at being in a hospital visible. He understood why the meeting had to be here, but he didn't have to like it. Especially since he'd been called back early from vacation. The time spent with his daughter was precious, even more so since it was limited to holidays and summer vacations. But he'd come anyway.

The elevator dinged and the doors opened. The scents and sounds were different here than the rest of the hospital. This was the private wing, and most of the money to build it had been donated by the MacKenzie family. It looked more like a hotel than a hospital—the walls were painted a soft green and the rooms were suites, so the families of the sick could be comfortable while they waited to see if their loved ones would live or die.

The carpet, soft and plush beneath his feet, silenced his steps, and he handed his security identification to the nurse at the front desk so she could scribble his name.

It had been eight weeks since an explosion had almost ended Shane MacKenzie's life just outside the MacKenzie Security compound in Surrender, Montana. The damage to his body had been terrible to witness, but Shane's cousin Thomas had managed to keep him alive until a helicopter could airlift him to the hospital. There'd been no possible way to save the leg that had been lost in the explosion. It had been a miracle he hadn't lost them both.

For six of those eight weeks Shane had been in a coma, every day a new roll of the dice. The swelling around the brain had worried the doctors more than anything, and they'd warned Shane's family that his mind might never be the same.

Archer had known Shane a few years now, and he couldn't imagine what the former Navy SEAL Commander was going through. Shane was meant for active duty, and according to Shane's older brother Declan—and Archer's boss—Shane wasn't fighting very hard to live.

The MacKenzie family had been taking turns at the hospital, making sure there was always a familiar face for Shane to see. Declan had set up a makeshift office in the little lounge area attached to Shane's room, and more often than not, there were other MacKenzies in and out as well. The security company was a family business after all, and Declan was the heart of it. Anyone who knew anything about MacKenzies understood that they always stood together, through the good times and the bad. And this definitely constituted as bad.

Dec had called while Archer had been lounging on a beach in Hawaii with his daughter, Stella. She'd just turned sixteen and was growing up before his eyes, and he'd wanted to give them both a memorable vacation before she started back to school the following week. He wouldn't have too many more years to enjoy her all to himself. She'd grown into a beautiful young woman, but she lived with her mother—his ex-wife—in Northern California, and between his job and her school schedule, their time together was much too infrequent.

The door that led into Shane MacKenzie's suite of rooms was open, but Archer knocked before he stepped inside. Declan MacKenzie sat behind a desk that had been set up in front of the group of windows that looked out on the parking lot. He commanded it as if hospitals were his normal place of business—his laptop open and the sleeves of his shirt rolled to the elbows as he talked softly into his cell phone.

The MacKenzies were all cut from the same cloth. When you saw the five siblings together, there was no doubt they were related. They all had hair as black as pitch and an arresting combination of physical features that made you look twice in their direction. Dec's eyes were gray as fog and one didn't have to look at them long to know that he wasn't a man to be messed with. The scar that ran along his jawline only added to the sense of danger.

Declan nodded at Archer when he came in the room and pointed to one of the chairs in front of the desk. Dec looked like a man who'd had too little sleep and too much worry.

It had been Declan's fiancé, Sophia, who Shane had been protecting when the missile had exploded. She was safe now, and the man who'd tried to kill her was dead, but Shane's future was still very much in the air.

Dec hung up the phone and leaned back in his chair with a sigh, rubbing his hand over his face.

"Thanks for coming," he said. "I'm sorry to cut your vacation short."

Archer settled back in his own chair and crossed his ankle over his knee. "I figured if you were calling me back from vacation, then it was probably important."

"How's Stella?"

"Pissed you cut her Hawaiian vacation short." Archer grinned at Dec. "She says you can make it up to her later though. She suggested you give me a raise so I can buy her the car she's been begging for."

Declan snorted out a laugh. "Christ, I can't believe she's driving. Seems like yesterday she was asking for piggyback rides."

"That's what happens when you get old. Don't worry, it won't be too long before you have your own kids asking for piggyback rides."

The look on Declan's face was content, despite the stress of the last weeks. He'd finally ended up with the woman he'd loved for years, and Archer was happy for his friend. Declan wasn't just his boss. Archer had worked many a black ops mission with Declan before they'd both decided to get out of the game. It had been a no brainer to follow Declan when he'd opened his own security company.

"How's Shane?" Archer looked to the connecting doorway that led to Shane's hospital room. The beep of monitors was soft and he could hear the low hum of the television in the background.

Dec's face said it all—the worry and anguish were plain to see. "His body is healing. The doctor said the area where they amputated is healing well. They were able to save the knee, which will be helpful when he's ready to wear a prosthetic. His other leg has had two surgeries already and pins were put in, but everything is looking fine there. They don't think he'll have to have any more surgeries on that leg, just a couple of skin grafts. The ribs are still giving him a little trouble, but the doctor said that was to be expected since they were cracked. His last brain scan was clear."

"But?"

Dec blew out a long breath. "He still isn't speaking. To any of us. He's shut himself off, just staring at the T.V. or the wall. My mother is in there with him now. She reads to him and talks to him. We all do. But he never responds. He won't talk to the trauma psychologist that keeps coming by or the doctors who monitor his progress."

"It's understandable, Dec. He's had his whole world taken from him. Commanding that team was his life. And he'll never lead them again."

"I know. And he's so fucking angry I just keep waiting for him to blow. You can't see it by looking at him, but I know my brother. His eyes are dead. I've seen men who had eyes like that, and nothing good came from it. And that terrifies me. His rage is festering beneath the surface, and until he lets it loose he'll never start to heal. At least on an emotional level. I don't know what to do for him."

For the first time Archer could recall, Declan looked helpless, and he had no idea what to do for his friend to make it better.

"You know I'll do whatever I can to help."

Dec pulled a file from beneath the massive stack of papers on his desk and tossed it to Archer. "Yeah, well, that's why I called you back early. I need to stay close by for now and I think you and I are the only two people suited to this job."

Meaning that the job required black ops training. Archer raised an eyebrow at that. "I'm listening."

"What do you know about Oblivion?"

"Just whispers really. Only that it exists. It's an off the books spook organization. The areas they work are murky at best and always dangerous. Even my security clearance didn't allow for much more information than that."

Dec nodded as if that's what he expected. "Three years ago, team members of Oblivion were contracted to find and terminate *Proteus*."

Archer let out a low whistle between his teeth and felt his adrenaline surge. He and Dec had both had run-ins with the terrorist known as *Proteus* in the past. They'd never won against him.

"Oblivion was able to link *Proteus* to a man named Francois Renard. Renard was a broker, and the one Proteus most often used. Somehow *Proteus* found out about the link and had Renard taken and held in an abandoned military base in France."

"A leak on the inside?"

"Suspected, but never proven. Oblivion knew Renard had been taken and had a team sent out to observe and assess whether an extraction was possible. It turns out *Proteus* was always a step ahead of the ops team. He'd planned that the team would try to rescue Renard and booby-trapped the whole place with explosives.

"It was run as a standard op. The scouts went in first, taking out guards and clearing the areas. Two agents were assigned to go in specifically for Renard and bring him out. Agents Jonah Salt and Audrey Sharpe."

"Oh, damn." Archer felt his blood run cold. Bits and pieces of what had happened on that mission had trickled to different parts of the agency. It was impossible to keep everything quiet. But they'd done a pretty good job of it. Whatever happened in France had been sealed and buried deep in the CIA vaults.

"Making a long story short, the base was blown to shit and so were most of the agents inside. A couple made it out with critical wounds. Salt and Sharpe had barely reached the perimeter when the blast went off, no doubt a timing miscalculation on *Proteus's* part or we'd have found their body parts along with the other agents. They made it out and managed to get back to their safe point to wait for extraction."

"I remember hearing about parts of this before they swept it under the rug." You couldn't belong to the agency without knowing who Jonah Salt was.

"Yeah. The two of them missed their meet for extraction, so undercover agents were dispatched to check out the scene and see what had gone wrong. They found Sharpe's body. She'd been shot three times in the chest and was hanging on by a thread when the team got there. The room had been ransacked and Salt was nowhere to be found. Sharpe died twice on the table during surgery."

"But she's alive?"

"She's alive. They never found Salt's body. His car went over the side of a cliff and there wasn't anything left to find. They pulled parts of the wreckage up, but there wasn't enough conclusive evidence to show tampering. There was, however, evidence of another car being involved, an extra pair of skid marks along with Salt's that went to the edge of the cliff. Someone knew who they were and hired a hit on both of them."

"Please tell me you didn't call me in to search for *Proteus*. I'm good, boss, but I think that's a job for more than one man."

"Hell, I'd trust you to take *Proteus* out before any of those new recruits they've replaced us with. Jesus, they're infants."

Archer grinned. It felt like they'd barely been older than that when they started.

"But no. That's not your assignment. I want you to bring in Audrey Sharpe."

Archer raised a brow in confusion. "Bring her in for what? Isn't she the agency's problem?"

"She resigned her position with the agency while she was still in the hospital recovering. And then as soon as she was able, she disappeared. Oblivion has been looking for her, but not with much enthusiasm. They never got to fully debrief her. They figured she was PTSD and it was best to let her go."

"What do you think?"

"I think she's as capable as ever. Her background is impressive. She was Mossad before she was recruited by the agency. *Kidon.*"

"Jesus. And they just let her go?"

"She'd been shot three times and left for dead. And that's after she'd already survived being tortured by the Syrians some years before. They thought she'd be ineffective."

"But you don't."

"No. I want her for MacKenzie Security. We need another

agent and she's more than qualified. And Oblivion might not be worried about what she knows, but she knows something. I've been following her pattern. She's hunting. Trying to stay off the grid as much as possible."

Declan smiled when he said it and Archer let out a short laugh. Dec could find anyone, anywhere. It didn't matter how off the grid they were.

"All of the information is in the file. You'll pick up her trail. Convince her to come back with you."

"And what about this personal mission she seems to be on?"

"Help her if need be. Or see if she'll abandon it altogether. We need her, and the sooner the better. I'm taking myself out of the field. The idea of being away from Sophia and a warm bed isn't all that appealing. And the business has reached the point where I do more good behind a desk than in front of it."

Archer ignored the pang of envy he felt whenever he looked at Declan. They'd shared similar lives and worked for the same organizations, but Archer didn't feel the same contentment that his friend did. His marriage had failed—because his wife couldn't handle not knowing about the secret missions and whether he'd come back alive—and he'd been young and arrogant enough to not bother trying to convince her that what they had was worth fighting and working for.

Now his daughter was being raised by another man. Granted, his ex-wife's husband seemed like a good guy and he was good to Stella, but Archer was jealous that the other man was the one getting to see his daughter grow into a woman.

But he'd blown his chance. Which was why Declan was sending him on this mission and not one of the other agents who had a family. He'd bring Audrey Sharpe back with him and then he'd go on the next mission, and then the next after that. And he wouldn't think about being content. He'd think about surviving.

"I'll bring her in for you," Archer finally said, grabbing the file and opening it. And then he felt the air whoosh out of his lungs and his heart pump faster. The photograph was taken from her CIA file, but there was nothing ordinary about the woman in it. Her face was clear of cosmetics or any enhancements, and still he had trouble believing what he was seeing.

Audrey Sharpe was the most breathtaking woman he'd ever laid eyes on. In the photo, dark hair was pulled back from an oval face. Her cheekbones were high, her chin slightly pointed, and her nose small and straight. Dark brows winged over almond shaped eyes the color of melted chocolate, and he felt his body stir as he scrutinized the photo and looked for flaws. There weren't any that he could see. Her lips were full and ripe and he wondered what they'd feel like against his skin. His cock spiked to full attention and his balls drew tight against his body, and he repositioned the file in his lap so he was covered.

"You've got to be fucking kidding me," he said, looking at Declan's amused grin. "No fucking way was this woman Mossad or a member of Oblivion. She'd stick out like a sore thumb."

"Don't be deceived by her looks. Mossad has a long history of recruiting beautiful and deadly women for just that purpose. I'd pit her skills against yours and mine any day."

"I have a feeling I'm going to hate this assignment." He'd never reacted to a woman, much less a photograph, like he had when looking at Audrey Sharpe. He couldn't imagine what the impact would be when he saw her up close and in person.

Archer turned the photo facedown, hoping to get the image of her out of his head, but there was another behind it. It took several seconds for him to comprehend what he was seeing.

"Jesus Christ." Where her face was a study in sheer beauty, her back was gruesome in its display of cruelty. Thick white scars marred almost every inch of skin where she'd obviously been flogged. Scars on top of scars. And along her ribs the skin was puckered where it had been burned.

"From her time with the Syrians," Declan explained. "She

didn't talk, so the torture went on for almost seventy-two hours before U.S. agents were able to extract her."

Cold fury slid through Archer at the thought of what she'd endured. But he turned to the next photograph, wanting—no needing—to see it all. The next photograph showed the front of her torso. The burn scars extended to the front of her ribs and just beneath her breasts, though her breasts remained untouched and smooth, making the scars seem all the more monstrous.

This photograph must have been the most recent, because three white bandages were placed over the wounds from where she'd been shot. It was a miracle the one in her upper chest hadn't pierced her heart.

Archer nodded and looked at Declan. "This much injury can damage the mind as well as the body."

Declan looked beyond him to the room where his brother lay. "Sometimes it can. But there are special people in the world that are worth pulling out of the abyss. I believe she'll be worth it."

"She's not going to want to come with me. If you say she's hunting, then she's got an agenda and nothing will make her stray from that."

Dec's lips twitched. "I guess that means you'll be helping her. Call me if there's trouble and I'll spare a couple of extra men, but I think she'll be more agreeable if it's just you. We wouldn't want to scare her off."

"A woman who's been tortured and left for dead isn't likely to scare easily."

Dec smiled again and the scar along his jaw tightened. "Just make sure you're not the one with your tail tucked between your legs at the end of it. MacKenzie Security has a reputation to uphold."

Archer shot Dec the finger, making him laugh. "It takes more than one woman to have me running scared."

Declan waited until Archer was out the door before murmuring, "We'll see, my friend. We'll see."

Also from Liliana Hart

THE MACKENZIE FAMILY SERIES

Dane

A Christmas Wish: Dane

Thomas

To Catch A Cupid: Thomas

Riley

Fireworks: Riley, *Coming July 1, 2014*

Cooper

1001 Dark Nights: Captured in Surrender

A MacKenzie Christmas

MacKenzie Box Set

Cade

Shadows and Silk

Secrets and Satin

Sins and Scarlet Lace

The MacKenzie Security Series (includes the 3 books listed above)

Sizzle

Crave, *Coming May 27, 2014*

THE COLLECTIVE SERIES

Kill Shot

THE RENA DRAKE SERIES

Breath of Fire

ADDISON HOLMES MYSTERIES

Whiskey Rebellion
Whiskey Sour - http://amzn.to/1jgoGgy
Whiskey For Breakfast - http://amzn.to/1fCl4kP
Whiskey, You're The Devil, *Coming August 5, 2014*

JJ GRAVES MYSTERIES

Dirty Little Secrets - http://amzn.to/OewCVt
A Dirty Shame - http://amzn.to/1c4ODdV
Dirty Rotten Scoundrel - http://amzn.to/MEacMl
Down and Dirty, *Coming November 25, 2014*

STANDALONE NOVELS/NOVELLAS

All About Eve
Paradise Disguised
Catch Me If You Can
Who's Riding Red?
Goldilocks and the Three Behrs
Strangers in the Night
Naughty or Nice

On behalf of 1001 Dark Nights,
Liz Berry and M.J. Rose would like to thank ~

Doug Scofield
Steve Berry
Richard Blake
Dan Slater
Asha Hossain
Chris Graham
Kim Guidroz
BookTrib After Dark
Jillian Stein
and Simon Lipskar

Printed in Great Britain
by Amazon